Christian!

THE SWORD OF
SIX WORLDS

So great to
meet you. I hope
you have an
excellent time
with Validus!

Matt Mikalatos

THE SWORD OF
SIX WORLDS

MATT MIKALATOS

Cappella
Books
Nashville, Tennessee

ISBN: 978-0-9882870-1-3

ISBN E-book: 978-0-9882870-0-6

Interior Design: Lisa Parnell, lparnell.com

Printed in the United States of America

19 18 17 16 15 14 13 12   1 2 3 4 5

This book is dedicated with much love
to my three daughters
—strong, brave, and true—

Zoey, Allie, and Myca

Chapter One

PATCHFACE
AND BENJAMIN

A crack at her window—so loud she thought the glass shattered—sent Validus Smith rolling off her rumpled bed and onto the floor. She had been in the middle of tying her shoes, her jeans and her favorite t-shirt already on. Another crack at the window, only this time Val saw what caused it. Someone was throwing rocks.

She crawled to the window and peeked over the white-painted sill to see her best friend Alex below, lifting another stone. His books were strewn on the ground at his feet—he always had lots of books—and a wide grin was plastered all over his face, or at least what she could see of it with his blond hair falling over his eyes. She pushed the window open.

"Alex Shields, put that rock down! Are you trying to break my window?"

He pushed the hair back from his face and called, "Did I scare you, Val?"

"No."

He grinned. "Looks like you just got up from the floor."

She smiled back at him. "I have strong reflexes. Go knock on the front door, and Mom will let you in. But don't tell her you were throwing rocks at the window!" Validus slung her backpack on and ran down the stairs.

Mrs. Smith opened the door and shuffled Alex to the breakfast table, straightening his shirt and making approving, clucking noises. He looked embarrassed by the attention. Mrs. Smith's hair was perfect, and she wore an apron. She looked like a mom from an old black and white TV show.

"Leave Alex alone, Mom."

Mrs. Smith swooped over and put her palm on Validus's forehead, just as Mr. Smith walked into the room, his thin hair sticking up and his round spectacles like owl eyes. "Good morning," he said cheerfully.

"Her temperature is normal," Mrs. Smith said, just as she said every morning and sometimes in the afternoon or before bed. "Tie your shoes, Val."

Mr. Smith poured himself a mug of coffee. "A normal temperature," he said with pride, as if Validus had taken top honors in her class. "Wonderful. Feeling like yourself today, then?"

Validus rolled her eyes. "Who else, Dad?"

He added a spoonful of sugar to his coffee, stirring as he sat up straighter in the chair. "Hard to say. For instance, I feel like an ancient Mesopotamian king."

Alex's eyes lit up. "Still working on your translation of *Gilgamesh*, sir?"

"Yes, my boy, yes! I've spent all morning reviewing my Akkadian grammar. What are you reading these days, my bookish friend?"

Alex pushed some toast in his mouth and pointed at a pile of books at his elbow. "The French knights of Charlemagne. Miss Holly suggested it. Interesting stuff."

Mr. Smith turned to his wife and said, "The Twelve Peers of Charlemagne! Did you hear that, dear? How thrilling."

Mrs. Smith frowned, looked to the clock, kissed Validus on the top of the head, and shooed them both out the door. "You're going to be late. Have a wonderful day at school, Validus! Good-bye, Alex! Remember, stay away from trouble, and trouble will stay away from you."

Mr. Smith crowded into the doorway and shouted after them, "Remember to watch your temper, Validus Smith!"

"Dad!" Validus sent a pointed glare back at her father, who smiled and waved. Validus and Alex turned down the sidewalk and headed toward the school. "Sorry about my parents. They're so . . ."

"Great?"

"I was going to say weird." She shrugged.

Alex laughed. "Maybe they're great if you don't live with them."

Just then Jeremy Lane walked up alongside them and said, "Hi, *Valerie*." Jeremy wore lumpy, oversized shirts and baggy jeans. His shoes looked as if they were worn through mud and weeds and never cleaned. His hair always looked like he just woke up. He had a round, red face, and he never missed a chance to bully those around him.

Validus took a deep breath, put her hands on her hips, and said calmly, "I've told you a hundred times, Jeremy, my name is Validus. From the Latin." That's what her parents said every time she complained about her name. More than once she told them the name was too weird. Each time they looked at each other in shock, and then Dad would say, "Honey, it's from the *Latin*."

Jeremy laughed for a long time. "Pig Latin," he said, and he punched Alex in the arm, hard. Validus bit the inside of her cheek and kept her clenched hands at her side. It took everything she had not to punch Jeremy herself, but Alex just rubbed his arm and shot Jeremy a dirty look.

They crossed onto school property, and Jeremy looked around carefully. Alex called out to a teacher and waved, to make sure Jeremy knew he was being watched. He sneered and walked away from them quickly and disappeared into the school. Alex pointed to the clock on the front of the building. He and Val hurried down the tiled hallway and into their classroom. Mom was right, they were almost late.

"Look," Alex said as they unloaded their books. "New kids." He tilted his head to the back of the classroom where a boy and girl stood nervously by the door. The boy scuffed the floor with one foot. His long, thin face was chestnut brown on the sides and forehead, but a shocking white patch extended across his nose and chin. *A burn mark, maybe*, Validus thought. His black hair fell past his shoulders. He didn't look like any other kid she had ever seen.

The girl had reddish orange hair and green eyes, and though her eyes were only half open, she seemed to be studying the classroom and the people in it. Both of the new kids looked as if they got dressed without parental approval. Their clothes didn't fit well. The boy's jeans were so long and baggy, the legs were cuffed three or four times to keep from dragging. The girl wore a long, green shirt tied up to keep it from looking like a dress.

The bell rang and a man, thin as an arrow, wrote his name on the board, his spidery fingers turning the chalk so it screeched. Mr. Jurgins. Validus sighed. She couldn't believe they had a substitute teacher. Miss Holly hardly ever missed a day of class, and she hadn't said anything about missing today. The substitute smiled sourly at the class. "That is my name." He looked over the classroom, his black eyes lingering momentarily on Validus. "We have two new students today, class. Sit down, children. Right there at the back, you two. That's fine. Now, your names are . . . Benjamin Gultiger?" He looked over his round glasses at the boy, who shook his head, his long hair covering his face.

"That's me, I think," the girl said.

Jeremy had slipped into the classroom just as the bell rang, out of breath and probably up to no good. He let out a loud guffaw and shouted. "Maybe you can be *Valerie's* boyfriend, Benjamin." Validus scowled at him. Jeremy had tried to think up other ways of mispronouncing Val's name, but he wasn't smart enough to come up with anything other than calling her Valerie. It could be worse. But the substitute didn't reprimand Jeremy, which was a bad sign. Jeremy Lane would be punching kids by the end of the day if he thought he could get away with it.

"You *think* your name is Benjamin?" Mr. Jurgins looked down his nose at the girl.

"Yes, that's me."

"So the girl is named Benjamin," Mr. Jurgins said. He looked at the boy with the brown and white face. "Then you must be, eh, Apul Lhusa?" Mr. Jurgins lowered the roll sheet and looked at the strange boy with the long black hair. The new kid nodded and blew the hair out of his face. "Answer me when I ask you a question." The boy cocked his head but didn't say anything.

"Maybe he only answers if you call him Patchface," Jeremy said, and his laughter rippled out into the rest of the classroom. Validus looked at Alex, who rolled his eyes and frowned. Alex had threatened more than once to punch Jeremy in the face, but Validus convinced him not to bother. "You'd just end up in the principal's office, and Jeremy would call you my boyfriend. It's not worth it."

Benjamin was sitting in the desk next to Jeremy, her green eyes still half closed, almost lazy. She leaned over and whispered something to Jeremy then smiled and showed off her perfect, tiny white teeth. Jeremy stopped laughing, and his face drained of color. His friends noticed, and they stopped laughing too. Then his face hardened, and he glared at Benjamin.

"No more talking in class, *Benjamin*," Mr. Jurgins sneered. Alex gasped, and Validus knew he was about to say how unfair it was when Mr. Jurgins turned to him and asked, "Have you something to add, Mr. . . . Shields, is it?" Alex didn't say anything, he just stared down at his desk.

Mr. Jurgins turned his attention to the boy with the white patch on his face. "Now. Would you prefer to be called Apul or Patchface?" Validus gasped this time, and Mr. Jurgins slowly turned his head toward her, the tip of his tongue flicking out. He looked like a snake smelling around for a mouse. Validus froze. No one spoke, not even Jeremy. "Well then. Patchface it is," Mr. Jurgins said. Validus felt her stomach drop into her shoes.

No one dared speak after that, and the morning dragged on slowly. Validus felt trapped, like being in a glass cage with that same snake. She rubbed her eyes. This whole thing felt unfair. Suddenly, Validus blurted out, "What happened to Miss Holly?"

Mr. Jurgins looked at Validus blankly, as if his eyes were having trouble focusing. Then one side of his mouth turned up into a smile. "I think you can stay in class during the break for speaking out of turn, Valerie. And don't think your precious Miss Holly can do anything about it. She won't be back."

Validus's face grew hot, but she remembered her father's warning to watch her temper and bit her lip to keep from saying what she wanted to say. Still, because she was going to miss her break anyway, she asked, "What happened to her?"

Mr. Jurgins turned his back and started to write on the board again. "Nothing, child. She couldn't stand the lot of you anymore, that's all." Then he laughed. A cold, mirthless laugh that sent chills up and down Validus's arms and made the hair on her neck stand up. She would rather be sent to the principal's office than sit with Mr. Jurgins during break. When it came she would bolt out the door and head for the far corners of the blacktop or the field. Validus saw that work once in a while for Jeremy.

But when break finally came, Mr. Jurgins stood with one thin finger on Validus's desk before announcing it. Then he bent over and whispered, "But you, little rat, will stay here with me." Validus's heart rapped against her chest, and she took a deep breath. She looked at Alex, who hesitated, deep concern in his eyes. But then Alex ran out the door with everyone else. There was nothing he could have done anyway.

Mr. Jurgins waited until the entire class was gone and then folded himself back-ward into the desk in front of Validus, so his pointy elbows were on the desktop and his strange diamond-shaped face and small black eyes were hanging just in front of Vali-dus's face. "You think you're the paladin of the universe, don't you, Miss Smith?" His breath was cold and papery. Validus wanted to scoot away from him, but she couldn't. She leaned as far back as she could, until her neck hurt, but Mr. Jurgins's face just seemed to follow her and to hang inches in front of her.

"I don't know that word," she said.

Jurgins laughed, but it was only a sound. His face didn't change. "The Universe, child. The earth, the sun, other earths and other suns, and the dark spaces between them. All that is one."

"The *other* word," she said, getting angry.

Mr. Jurgins turned his head sideways and a little away, sizing Validus up. "Don't play games with me, Miss Smith. I know you're the paladin. They'll find your little broken body somewhere on the field, just like Miss Holly. And don't think any help is coming. Silverback and his Breakers have shattered the Sword of Six Worlds."

The air pushed out of Validus's chest. She didn't understand everything Jurgins was saying, but the threat was clear enough. "They'll catch you. You'll go to jail."

"Jail," Mr. Jurgins said, dismissing it. "I'll be gone. Home in my own cozy little universe and a hero for disposing of a paladin. We can't have you coming into our world and causing problems."

"I'm not a . . . whatever you said."

"A paladin? A palace guard? A knight-errant? Hmmmm. I might believe you. Nevertheless, it would be safer for me to kill you. Maybe your little friend Alex is the paladin. I know it's someone in this class, or your Miss Holly wouldn't have denied it so vehemently." His hands struck out so fast Validus didn't even see them move. He pinned her arms tight. He opened his mouth wide, and two long fangs dropped down from the roof of his mouth. Validus could see dark slits from where they dropped. Mr. Jurgins's jaw sagged lower than Validus would have thought possible and then the door flew open and banged against the wall, and Alex was standing there, breathless. "Mr. Jurgins," he said. "Come quick. There's a fight. The principal is asking for you."

The thing holding Validus snapped its mouth shut and was Mr. Jurgins again. He unfolded himself and took long strides out the door, but not before giving Validus a look of pure hatred. "We'll finish our business later," he growled. Then he brushed past Alex and was gone.

"C'mon, Val, we have to get out of here before he finds out I lied."

Alex pushed Val's jacket into her hands, and they went around the building the opposite way from Mr. Jurgins, headed for the far corners of the field, where teachers rarely visited. They sat down against the school sign.

Validus shuddered. "Did you see his fangs, Alex?" Alex shook his head, so she told him everything that had happened. "I'm not going back in there. You shouldn't either." She thought for a minute. "No one should go back in there."

Alex shrugged. "We can't skip class. He'll just call the principal, and then we'll get in trouble before he eats us."

Validus noticed Apul. He was hard to miss with that great white mark down the center of his face. He was sprinting full speed around the blacktop, throwing his head so his long black hair whipped in the breeze. No one was chasing him or playing with him, he just seemed to be running for the sake of running. Then she saw Benjamin crouched next to a game of four square, as if she was about to spring into the middle of it, her green eyes following the movement of the ball. Suddenly she pounced, pinning the red rubber ball to the pavement. A cry rose from the four square kids, followed by shouting and pointing, and finally Benjamin crouched outside the square again, her eyes following the ball.

"Hey!" Alex said and jumped to his feet. "Apul, look out!" Validus scrambled up after him just in time to see Jeremy with a big stick, and two of his buddies were distracting Apul so Jeremy could trip him. It worked perfectly. Validus heard the smack of the stick against Apul's shins, like the sound of a baseball bat hitting a ball. Apul fell to the ground and skidded across the pavement, and soon everyone was running.

Alex was halfway to Apul by the time Validus started moving, but Benjamin was faster than both of them. As Validus ran she saw Mr. Jurgins appear beside Apul. He caught Validus's eye and smiled. Validus suspected Mr. Jurgins wasn't planning to punish Jeremy. This was her chance to walk away from the whole thing. She could call her mom, tell her she had a temperature, and be home in no time. Or she could try to help the new kids and protect her classmates from Mr. Jurgins. She gulped and poured on more speed.

Chapter Two

IN THE PRINCIPAL'S OFFICE

Jeremy's smirk made Validus sick. Apul groaned, lying on the ground and holding his shins. Jeremy twirled the stick he had used to knock him down. "I'm sooooo sorry," Jeremy said, while Alex helped Apul to his feet.

Alex's face flushed red. "You did that on purpose, Jeremy."

Jeremy grinned.

Benjamin slipped Apul's arm over her shoulder. "Are you okay?" she asked. Apul didn't say anything, just let a burst of air push past his lips. Benjamin turned to Jeremy. "Did you use a stick? That's what he said, that you hit him in the leg with a stick."

"Shut up, *Benjamin*. He didn't say anything you dumb girl-boy." Jeremy's face turned bright red. It looked as if it might pop.

Mr. Jurgins stopped him with a gesture. "I saw the whole thing." He rested his hand on Jeremy's shoulder, whose face went quickly from a bright red to a sickly green. "Miss Smith will accompany me to the principal's office to explain her actions."

Jeremy looked confused, but it didn't take more than a heartbeat for him to take advantage of the situation. His face brightened, and he nodded. "Good thing I got this stick away from her before she could hit anyone else."

Jurgins plucked the stick from his hands. "You are the hero of the hour. The rest of you, back to the classroom. Miss Smith and I will walk to the principal's office." Validus could see the shocked looks on Alex's and Benjamin's faces. Apul looked thoughtful, his big dark eyes watching Jurgins without blinking.

"I should go to the office, too," Alex said carefully. Validus felt a rush of affection for Alex. He was a good friend, and she was glad she wouldn't be alone with Mr. Jurgins.

"No need for that," Jurgins said. Mr. Jurgins had his hand on Validus's shoulder now, and it was like a claw tearing into her skin. She bit her lip. This might be it, then, and she didn't even understand what was going on. She looked up and saw Mrs. Stevens walking toward them, her huge body swaying beneath her floral dress. She was the meanest teacher at the school. Nothing went unpunished. In that respect, she was fair. Overly fair.

"Mrs. Stevens!" Validus shouted, and as soon as Alex heard her name, a smile came across his face. He beamed at Mr. Jurgins.

"It looks like I'm going to the principal's office after all," Alex said. With that he kicked the substitute in the shins as hard as he could.

"MR. SHIELDS!" Mrs. Stevens roared, still ten feet away. "You are going to the principal's office for that."

"No need for that," Mr. Jurgins said, grimacing. "He was only playing."

"Zero tolerance, sir. I won't allow rule breaking. I see there has been a problem with Miss Smith as well. I'll take them both to Principal Rita. How about these two? New students, aren't you? What's the problem?"

"Jeremy Lane hit my friend with a stick," Benjamin said.

Mrs. Stevens's eyes narrowed. "That's no surprise. Is that him way over there by the classrooms?" She took a breath so deep Validus knew to cover her ears before the deafening, "JEREMY!" echoed across the blacktop. Every kid on the playground stopped in midstep. Jeremy dragged his feet and slowly made his way to them. Validus's shoulder was starting to hurt from Mr. Jurgins's fingers digging in.

"I didn't hit the stupid Patchface," Jeremy said when he finally got over to them. "He tripped."

Without warning, Benjamin leapt across Mrs. Stevens and knocked Jeremy to the ground. Validus could hardly see what happened next, but she had the bare impression of a blur of reddish orange hair, Benjamin on Jeremy's chest, and then blood on Benjamin's face and shirt and all over Jeremy's neck. Then it was over, and Benjamin was hanging by the scruff of her neck from Mrs. Stevens's fat hand and smiling so all her sharp white teeth showed. Jeremy was bawling, and Benjamin snapped, "I warned you to stay away from Apul or else. I keep my promises."

Jeremy wailed and rolled on the ground. Validus felt light-headed from all the blood, but she wasn't even sure what had happened. Mr. Jurgins helped Jeremy to his feet. Jeremy had one hand clamped over the side of his neck and a murderous look in his eye, but he stayed well away from Benjamin.

Mrs. Stevens clucked and shook her head. "I'm taking all five of you to the principal."

Mr. Jurgins rubbed his hands together quickly, and his tongue darted out to lick his lips. "I can take them over myself."

"And who will watch your class? If you can't get what remains of that class into their room and studying quietly by the time I bring these five back, this will be your last time as a substitute. We don't appreciate teachers who encourage disobedience and lawlessness. Off you go. Shoo."

To Val's amazement, Mr. Jurgins obeyed. He looked over his shoulder with narrowed eyes, but Validus guessed Mrs. Stevens had bought them half an hour out of the classroom and out of Mr. Jurgins's reach. Mrs. Stevens grabbed Jeremy by the collar and yanked him in the direction of the principal's office.

Alex fell in next to Validus, and they gave each other tentative smiles. "Thanks, Alex.

You didn't have to get yourself in trouble like that."

"I'd rather go to the principal's office than back into the classroom with that *thing*." He sighed. "I wish Miss Holly would come back."

Benjamin grabbed Validus's and Alex's elbows and pulled them a few steps farther behind Mrs. Stevens, who looked over her shoulder and gave them a don't-try-any-thing-funny-because-I've-been-teaching-here-for-thirty-years look. Benjamin whispered, "What do you mean by *thing*?"

She probably wouldn't believe it. But Benjamin might be in as much danger as Validus, and she didn't want to feel guilty if the new kid got eaten. "He's—" The words stuck in her throat. *He's a monster. He has fangs and eats people.* "He kept asking me if I was a palace inn or a palid-something when he kept me in from break." Benjamin's eyes widened. "Don't let him be alone with you, that's all," Validus finished lamely.

"He thinks you're the paladin?" Benjamin asked. Apul trotted closer to them. Benjamin's grip on Val's arm tightened, and she pulled her to a stop. "Then you're the one we're here to find. I didn't think the paladin would be a cub. I assumed it would be one of the teachers."

Alex and Validus practically stepped on each other trying to ask her what she was talking about. Benjamin's eyebrows shot up. She looked to Apul, who shook his head in disbelief. "Haven't they started your training yet?"

"I don't know anything. In fact, Mr. Jurgins said maybe Alex was the paladin instead of me."

Benjamin looked at Alex, who shook his head. "I don't know anything, either, except that in my books a paladin is a kind of knight. And we should all stay away from Mr. Jurgins."

"Is he different than your other teachers?" Benjamin asked.

Validus laughed. "Different than other human beings, I think."

"Grumbacher," Apul said.

"Then they're already here," Benjamin said.

Mrs. Stevens came back and took Validus and Alex gently by the necks and steered them into the school office, eventually directing them to a stiff-backed plastic bench. Apul and Benjamin followed and sat across from them.

"Jeremy is talking with Principal Rita right now," Mrs. Stevens said. "I'm going in there to hear what he has to say for himself. You four had best be on those benches when I get back."

In any case, sneaking away seemed impossible. A secretary whose name Validus didn't know sat at a wide, black desk just inside the next room, angled so she could see the benches with a quick glance up from her computer. Validus sighed and unzipped her jacket. If Mr. Jurgins didn't murder her, her parents would. She had never had a call home from the principal and definitely not for fighting. The look on Alex's face was even worse. He never broke the rules, and Validus was surprised that he lied even to save her life. Alex tried to keep his parents completely out of things, and Validus had only met them once. She knew it would be Alex's worst nightmare to have them called into the principal's office.

She didn't understand most of what had happened today. Her mouth was dry, her palms were sweating, and she was starting to feel sick to her stomach.

"Hey," Benjamin whispered. "We have to leave now. If one of you is the paladin, we need your help."

Validus frowned at Benjamin. "What are you talking about? The only place we're going is the principal's office."

Apul walked idly around the room, his back to the walls, tapping on them with the flat of his foot. His head was turned to one side, as if he was listening for something. He wore a thick, white anklet on his left leg—

it flashed blue as he tapped it against the wall. Benjamin glanced at Apul then at the secretary. "A renegade group of our people are trying to break into a Locked World, to release a deadly force called the Blight. Our own paladin was killed or captured when he went to investigate, along with an entire group of our warriors. The Twelve Peers of Earth sent your paladin to help us, but we haven't heard from her for three weeks, and now the enemy claims they've destroyed the Sword of Six Worlds, which is bad news for all of us."

"If it's true," Apul said.

Benjamin nodded. "One of you is the next in line to be paladin of *this* universe. Our world is only one rotation from yours, only one door down. You have to help us, it's in all our treaties, and it's in your interest to keep the Blight from spreading. If they succeed in opening a Locked World, it's only a matter of time before they try to destroy your world. You *must* come."

Validus whistled through her teeth, without a tune. Benjamin's speech didn't make things any clearer. Alex had that look on his face he always got when he was concentrating hard: top teeth biting his lower lip, his eyebrows almost touching above his nose.

Apul leaned over Benjamin. "They haven't even sworn the oath." He looked at Validus and Alex through his long, black hair, the white patch of his face bright behind it. "They're *children*. What can they do against the Blight? Or the mad winds? Or even Silverback if it comes to that? We've failed. Let these children live their lives in peace."

"A short peace to go with a short life," Benjamin hissed back at him. The secretary looked up sharply, and Benjamin smiled politely. The secretary's eyes dropped reluctantly to her computer. As soon as her eyes were off them, Benjamin put one hand on Validus's knee and one on Alex's. "I know you don't understand. Come with us, and we will have time to explain."

The intensity of Benjamin's green-eyed stare made Val nervous. She hoped the principal would come out soon. She felt safe from Mr. Jurgins here in the office. She was about to tell Benjamin to leave them both alone when Alex asked softly, "How long will we be gone?"

Benjamin looked down at the floor. "A week. Two at the most."

Apul snorted. "At least tell them the truth."

She looked back up at them. "Our best warriors have not returned, including two paladins. We may not survive. It may be the four of us against the Blight."

"The four of us?" Alex said. "But you're just kids, too."

Benjamin said something after that, but Validus didn't hear it. She was distracted by something else, a strange stirring beside her, like a winter draft in a cabin. A fern on a stand beside her shivered. Then Validus heard a faint whisper over her right shoulder. "You are the paladin," it said. She turned to look but found no one. Goosebumps stood up on her arm. Maybe it was her imagination. But no, she had heard it quite clearly. When she looked back, Alex and Benjamin were staring at her. "Can I say good-bye to my parents?" she asked, surprising herself.

As if in answer, Apul trotted back to them and said quietly, "I've found a thin place in the wall. It's time to go." He pulled his pant leg up slightly, and the thick anklet was glowing a soft green. Benjamin nodded and told him to make a hole. The thin place was just under the large window looking out over the blacktop and parking lot. Anyone who was coming to the principal's office had to pass that window—which was how much time they had when they saw Mr. Jurgins's pasty white face stop by the window and turn toward them. His eyes locked on Validus, and she knew whatever rules kept Jurgins from killing her in front of an audience had been lifted. He scowled, then he disappeared as he hurried toward the office door. "I'll come last," Apul said, and with a tremendous backward kick he bashed a hole in the wall.

The door to the office flew open, and Mr. Jurgins dashed in, growling. Principal Rita threw open her door, her face an enraged purple. The secretary called to see what was wrong, and Apul bent over the small hole he had made in the wall. A slight cinnamon-scented breeze sighed into the room through the hole, which went completely through the wall. Instead of sunshine, pale moon-light shone on the other side. In any other situation Validus would have hesitated, but with Mr. Jurgins and Principal Rita on either side of her, the hole seemed a sensible option. Still, the hole was barely the size of a baseball, and although it grew every time Apul's anklet pulsed from green to a bright golden, it was not growing fast enough.

"Stop!" Mr. Jurgins yelled, just as Principal Rita demanded to know what was going on. Jurgins grabbed Apul and knocked him against the wall, and his glowing anklet broke into several pieces. Benjamin cried out, leapt onto the floor, and widened the hole with her fingers. It stretched and tore, like a rip in a t-shirt. Benjamin pushed Alex toward the hole, and Val gasped as his head, then his body, and lastly his sneakers disappeared. Benjamin grabbed Val's hand. Mr. Jurgins lifted Apul over his head. Benjamin shoved Validus into the hole, which stretched and gave way, but it was tight, like putting on last year's Christmas sweater. She couldn't breathe for one terrible moment, and for a split second saw a long, white corridor filled with doors. Then she spilled out onto the cool soil on the other side.

"Over here," Alex whispered. He was behind a rock the size of a diesel truck. Validus crawled beside him. She could still see sunlight through a rip in the night air. A plate-sized hole that led back into the school office hung in the air in front of them. "Get down," Alex said. "If Ben and Apul come through they'll find us quickly enough, and if it's Mr. Jurgins—" He shuddered. "We should hide as well as we can."

Validus slid down beside him. She tried not to think about what might be coming through the hole. She took a deep breath and then looked at the area in front of them. It looked like a wheat field, but it was bright blue in the moonlight. Plants grew waist-high as far as she could see. They were hiding behind the giant rock, the only different thing in the whole place. The moon hung in front of them, pale and swollen. Val's hands trembled. She looked more closely. Her hand was casting two shadows, one toward her and one onto the ground. She looked straight up and saw another moon overhead, bright and hard and small.

"What have we gotten ourselves into, Alex?"

"Shhh. I think I heard Benjamin say something on the other side of the rock." Validus held her breath. Her heart was beating hard, but after a few deep breaths to calm herself she could clearly hear the labored breathing of a large animal. Alex's eyes widened. Validus got his attention, put a finger to her lips, then snuck quietly to the top of the rock and peeked over. It *was* an animal. It was the biggest tiger she had ever seen. And it was sniffing the ground, heading for the far side of the rock, directly toward Alex.

Chapter Three

THE GRUMBACHER

Validus had never seen a tiger in the wild. Its great orange and black head was twice the size of her own, and its tail was longer than her legs. The tail twitched with nervous energy as the big cat slipped through the moonlight. It gave a low growl and moved toward Alex's side of the rock.

Validus didn't dare call to him because she knew the tiger would hear and bound to the top of the rock in half a second. For one horrible moment she thought the tiger wouldn't be hungry once it finished with Alex, and if she let it eat him she could get away. The shame washing over her gave her strength for what she did next.

She scrambled around the edge of the rock until she was moving alongside the tiger. She could see it ten feet below her, head low to the ground. She leapt, aiming for the center of its back, hoping with all her heart that its back might break when she hit it.

She tried not to make a sound, but halfway down she let loose a terrifying cry, giving the tiger a half second to shift its weight, rolling partially out of her way. She landed in a heap on top of the cat, but she knew she barely hurt it. The cat swiped her in the head with one enormous paw, sending her sprawling into the waist-high wheat. She scuttled backward, deeper into the wheat, and hoped her scream had warned Alex.

Then she heard Benjamin's voice. "Validus, I need your help. Come quickly!"

She licked her lips and debated whether to answer, but she couldn't allow the tiger to eat Benjamin because she was afraid to speak up. She raised her voice and called, "Benjamin, be careful! There's a tiger out there."

The tiger's head parted the wheat in front of her. "If you don't hurry," the tiger said, "there will be more terrifying things than tigers here." Val's mouth fell open. The tiger spoke with Benjamin's voice. "Hurry," it snapped, and Validus brushed her jeans off and followed. She ran around the rock and slid to a stop in front of the bright hole, which led back to the principal's office.

"When Apul comes through," Benjamin said, "you need to close the hole. Jurgins broke our swidgel stick, so you'll need to gather the edges in your hands, clamp them together, and then tie it in a knot." Validus stammered something, but even as she said it she knew it made no sense. "I would do it, but I don't have hands anymore. And just when I was getting used to them." Benjamin crouched by the hole. "Here he comes."

Validus moved closer to the hole, her hands up and ready to grab the edges. Apul's face appeared on the other side, about to push through, but what came out was not Apul's face. A huge black nose the size of

Val's fist, so large it filled the whole opening, pushed its way through, then the hole stretched to allow the bulk of the creature's head out. The long face followed, brown and white with a black mane, and then its neck, which grew in thickness as it came out of the hole. The hoofed feet and barrel chest of a horse closely followed. Its midsection seemed to have taxed the hole to its absolute limits, and the horse's front feet scrabbled at the soft ground, trying to pull itself forward and out of the hole. "Quickly," the horse said. "Widen the hole."

She stepped up to the horse's side and squeezed her fingers into the hole, leaning back with all her weight until she felt it start to stretch. The horse strained forward, and at last his midsection was through. His hindquarters followed, and he stepped lightly away from the hole.

Benjamin yelled, "Close it, Validus!"

Validus stepped in front of the hole, grabbed a side in each hand then pulled it toward herself. The hole puckered out toward her like an overstuffed trash bag, but it felt as if enough give existed to tie it together, just like Benjamin said. But then she saw Mr. Jurgins's leering face on the other side, his hand stretched toward her. Validus stumbled back and almost lost her grip on the edge.

The thing that came out of the hole wasn't a hand at all but a flat, segmented tentacle as wide as Val's chest and pasty white. It looked like a gigantic tape worm. It wrapped itself around Val's arm and started to yank her back toward the hole. Validus cried out for help. An orange and black flash bounced in front of her, and one snap of her jaws severed the tentacle from the creature.

Validus yanked the hole hard and twisted and tied until she couldn't see light from the other side. She waved her hand through the space, but it was only air now. She fell back onto the ground, exhausted. Only then did she realize that part of the tentacle was still wrapped around her arm. With a cry she unwound it and threw it as far as she could, out into the wheat. Round, angry red spots appeared on her arm where it had touched her. She felt nauseous. She shivered when she thought about the worm-thing touching her.

Validus heard a commotion from the direction she had thrown it, so she stood shakily and moved into the wheat. Apul was stomping the wheat flat, and Benjamin was leaping back and forth, tearing at the ground with her claws. "Here!" she cried, digging furiously into the ground, clods of dirt spraying up behind her and caking Val's mouth and hair. She spit out some dirt and moved to the side.

Benjamin's paws were a blur of orange, dirt flying past with startling speed. A hole rapidly formed, and Benjamin leapt into it to continue digging. Validus leaned over the edge and saw a wiggling white strand that managed to stay just out of Benjamin's reach. It dug faster than Benjamin, and after a few moments she slowed. She took a few more halfhearted swipes at the dirt before jumping out of the pit and shaking the soil off her fur. She flopped onto the ground, her sides heaving.

"We should move for the Citadel," Apul said gruffly, nudging Benjamin in the side with a hoof. Benjamin stretched out so she could see him clearly with her bright green eyes, and she yawned so wide that Validus could see all her teeth. Her tongue lagged out, and she watched Apul without saying anything. He snorted. "That grumbacher will be after us in a few hours."

"You're such a pessimist," Benjamin said, getting lazily to her feet. "They usually grow back slower than that." She rolled her eyes to look at Validus, as if she should have known better than to throw the tentacle away. "For future reference, *Paladin*, you cannot toss grumbacher tentacles away and be rid of them. It will grow a new head and body in about half a day. Their memories aren't completely coherent at first, so they hunt whatever they had the most recent taste of. Which, in this case, would be you."

"What should I have done?" Validus shivered and looked around, half expecting to see it lurking in the moonlight.

"Put it in a bag of blood," Benjamin said. "Then it won't regenerate. Put it on a lesser animal." She paused and looked to see if she understood. "A lesser animal is one that doesn't speak." She sighed. "Some paladins keep them attached to themselves until they find a fire hot enough to consume the grumbacher completely, but I wouldn't suggest that."

"What's the best thing to do?"

"You'll get a chance to answer that question in half a day," Apul said. He looked to Benjamin. "We would make better speed without her."

Validus put her hands on her hips. "What's that supposed to mean?"

"He means," Benjamin said softly, "that he doesn't think you are a paladin and therefore not of use. He means we should abandon you in an unfamiliar world and trust you to find your way through grumbachers and swadzels and worse." She turned to the horse, and when she spoke this time Validus heard a low growl in the back of her throat. "It sounds like a mad wind speaking to me."

"Sacrifice a foal to save the herd," Apul said.

Benjamin shook her head as if trying to shake off a fly. "Without hands or a swidgel stick, how would you have closed that hole?"

"If we hadn't come for the child, we wouldn't have lost that swidgel stick. Crackbeak will not be pleased."

"Crackbeak knew the risks. This child saved your life. We will not abandon her. We find Alex and then we head for the Citadel. Together."

Apul snorted. "It's your hide, not mine. I'll be on the western road, along the Wide River." He trotted off into the moonlight, straight through the field.

Benjamin nudged Validus in the back with her head. "Let's find Alex and be on our way." She walked lazily over toward the big rock, sniffing the ground here and there. She turned her green eyes on Validus, waiting for her. She was still watching the tiny silver wake that Apul made through the wheat. "You mustn't judge him harshly. His story is more tragic than you know." She paused. "He saved your life, too, when he found the thin place between our worlds and opened the passageway."

Validus nodded. "We hid on the far side of the rock," Validus said. "I guess Alex slipped into the wheat when he heard me yell."

They couldn't find a trace of him. Benjamin sniffed all around where they had been sitting and said the scent was strong, but she couldn't find a sign that he had left. Validus called for him a few times before Benjamin warned her to drop her voice. The stalks of wheat all around the rock were unbroken, except where Validus had been.

Benjamin flopped to the ground, her front paws crossed. Validus had never personally known a tiger, but she looked deep in thought. At last Benjamin stood. "I think the Rock of Many Names has invited Alex into its heart. Come. We may still be able to catch our cranky horse friend."

"We can't just leave Alex. How could a rock invite him to do anything?"

"Walk with me, and I will explain." When Validus didn't move, Benjamin pushed her forehead into Val's chest until she started to fall backward. She took a step in the direction Benjamin wanted her to go, and soon she was walking down Apul's trail, looking back every few steps at the rock, which rose from the wheat like a golden island, the moonlight glancing off it like spears.

"Is he safe?" Validus asked.

"That I cannot say. But he is beyond our reach."

Chapter Four

THE ROCK
OF MANY NAMES

Alex heard the strange panting of a large animal. Validus scrambled up the rock, and then he couldn't hear her at all. He stood with his palms against the boulder's cool side, listening intently. For one brief instant, Val stood at the edge of the rock, silhouetted against the moon, and then she jumped, shouting as she fell. At that moment Alex's hands sank into the rock, as if he were leaning on an enormous mound of softened butter. He let out a small yelp, and then he fell forward, through the rock and onto the ground.

The moonlight, in fact all the light, disappeared. The fall had knocked his breath out. The floor and the walls were made of smooth, unyielding stone. He caught his breath then stood and paced out the chamber. It was circular, about ten feet around. He yelled as loud as he could, which was just loud enough to hurt his ears and, he suspected, not loud enough to be heard by Validus outside the stone.

Alex moved around the walls, leaning on them with two flat palms, thinking maybe he had triggered a trap door or secret passageway. He could find no evidence of a way out. He knew he could survive three days before he would die from thirst, but he might run out of air even sooner. He decided he shouldn't scream or exert himself, so he sat down against the wall and waited.

Time passed slowly in complete darkness, and he found his imagination taking unpleasant liberty with thoughts about other things sharing his dark chamber. He closed his eyes and felt a hairy tickling on his neck, exactly the sort of feeling he would expect from a tarantula. He leapt up from the wall and turned toward it. Two bright flames suddenly lit the room. He swiped his hand at them, thinking they were the eyes of some fabulous spider, but his hand passed directly between them.

The two flames brightened, and he could see a narrow, stone staircase leading deeper into the stone. The passageway wasn't there a moment before, he was certain of that, and he worried that it would close again with him inside it if he followed the lights, which were hovering expectantly at the lip of the stairs.

"At least stairs go somewhere," he mumbled. He stepped onto the first stair. The flames bobbled excitedly and dropped several feet down the corridor. Alex took a deep breath and followed them. His mind kept wandering to books he had read where dark, stone corridors were filled with ancient skeletons. He found he could keep from thinking about a bony hand falling onto his shoulder if he focused on the flames.

After a few minutes, the stairs took a sudden spiral dive. It continued down, down, and around in a tight, continual blind curve. He continued through the cool, damp corridor, and over and over he asked himself, *What could be around this next corner?*

Every step revealed a new bit of the tunnel ahead, a new opportunity for imagining horrible creatures, lurking darknesses, spiders, snakes, and skeletons. He forced himself to think more positively. "Maybe there's a big slice of cake around the corner," Alex said to himself. "Or a horse. A pile of gold. A library. Validus. A way out of here."

The lights darted around the corner now, picking up speed. Alex had to move twice as fast to keep up. He didn't want to be left alone in the dark. It would be worse, somehow, now that he had seen the light for a short time. They were too fast, though, and soon he was chasing their faint afterglow rather than the flames themselves.

"Wait!" he called. "I'm still following you." To his relief the light got brighter, which he took to mean they had slowed and were waiting for him. He turned the corner, gasped, and stopped. The passageway widened into a large chamber with pale, multicolored stalactites and stalagmites never touched by the sun. Gemlike sparkles winked from dark corners. A breath of chilled air touched his skin, and he heard the distant plink of dripping water. A multitude of small flames hung like globes along a long ceiling, which dripped with water and stone.

An enormous boulder sat in the center of the chamber, a lump that looked like a man's back, though at least twice the size of an ordinary man. Then, to Alex's horror, the rock *moved*. It turned toward him, the stone back giving way to an enormous stone chest. A ponderous head sat on its shoulders, with black holes where the eyes should be and no nose at all. The mouth was little more than a fissure in the rock face.

Alex carefully stepped backward and felt for the stairs with his feet, never taking his eyes off the thing in the chamber. But the stairs were gone. He felt behind him with his hands and felt a rock wall, cold and wet and much closer than it should be.

The rock-thing stood, towering over him, its head bent in his direction. It lifted a hand toward him, and then the fissure on its face opened wider.

"Don't be frightened of the flames," it said, its voice rumbling like an avalanche. "They are quite tame."

Alex tried to say something but couldn't. He rested his back against the rock wall and lowered himself to the ground.

The rock-thing looked back to the globes of light hanging in the cavern. "I caught them myself. They won't harm you." It turned to him again, watching him carefully. It made a low humming noise. "You are still frightened. I will put out the lights."

"No!" Alex's voice echoed over and over through the cavern.

The stone-thing turned, as if watching his voice bounce from wall to wall. It seemed amused. It didn't speak again until Alex's voice died away and the almost-silence of the dripping water returned.

"I had forgotten how noisy you little things are," it rumbled. It moved back to the center of the room and beckoned for him to follow. It sat in roughly the same place it had been and then put its hands straight through the floor, as if the stone were made of water. It pulled up a perfectly formed stone chair and set it beside him. It reached into the floor again and pulled up a table. "Sit," it said. "You can't eat my food. But I can give you some refreshment."

It stirred the table with its thick forefinger and pulled up. A swirled stone cup followed his finger from the tabletop. It was empty when Alex first looked inside but soon began filling from the bottom with clear water. He gratefully took a sip, and it was sweet and cool. He drained the cup. Water immediately pooled up within it when he set it down again. The table was completely smooth except for one tiny catch in the rock.

The creature apparently saw Alex looking at it because it reached across the table and smoothed it out. When its giant hands came near him, Alex flinched. The creature pulled back in surprise. "Not afraid of my pets after all. Afraid of me. Ha ha. And after I saved you. That won't do."

It swirled up a big cup for itself, dipped its fingers into the cup, and dripped water from its fingers onto its head. It did this several times. "Helps me think," it said. It was silent for about a minute.

Alex took another drink, not knowing what to do and too scared to speak.

"Once I sat beneath a stalactite for a century, just thinking. When I moved around again I'd grown a pointy cap. Ha ha ha. From the water dripping on me, you see.

"I'm trying to remember what to do for scared little animals. I think it was . . . yes, there was a list. Let them know they can trust you, that was the first rule. Tell them your story was number two. Number three was . . . hmm . . . what was it? Ah. Let them give you a name. That's right. My training was a long time ago. Hmmm. You *can* trust me you know."

Alex almost laughed. The rock-thing wasn't so frightening now, the way it rambled on. On the other hand, he was still trapped underground. "I could trust you a lot more if you would let me out of this cave. I'd rather be outside."

The rock harrumphed. "There's a grumbacher out there, you know. That's why I pulled you inside, I saw it coming."

"What's a grumbacher?"

The rock rumbled, deep in its chest. "Nasty creatures. Servants of the Blight."

"Is Validus still out there with it? Is she okay?"

"I would have brought your friend in, too, but she jumped off of me just as I went to get you. There was a large cat, too. I could see you are important people, what with a grumbacher chasing you. Up to no good, those things. I always collapse on them if they burrow too close." It leaned close to him, its massive elbows on the table.

Alex had the frightening sensation the rock-man was going to fall on him, like a pile of bricks.

"Your friend and the cat have moved off to the west and are safe for the moment." It paused. "It is rude, by the way, "to say you don't like it inside someone's heart."

Alex got out of his chair and backed away. It could smash him in a moment, and he had offended it. He should have known better than to open his mouth. As he always told himself the first week of the school year, "Keep quiet for four days, and the teacher won't hear you on day five."

The rock sighed. "I've frightened you again. I was only explaining that in my culture what you said was rude. The training said to be honest but patient. Don't creep away like that. I think we should skip ahead to giving me a name. Yes, I think that would be more helpful than a story, don't you? Sit down, sit."

Alex returned to his seat.

"Good. The trick is to find a name that won't be frightening. For instance, in this world the local people call me the Rock of Many Names. In the next world over they call me Deathbringer. Maybe that would be a good name." It lifted a hand to its head. "Your face has changed colors. White as chalk."

"I don't think Deathbringer is the right name," Alex said. "Maybe you could tell me your real name."

The rock nodded and mumbled various affirmatives. Suddenly, the whole cave shook. Alex grabbed the stone table and held on until his knuckles turned white. Dust spilled into the cavern, and the floor rippled like a wave in a pool. Water sprayed up from the small cavern puddles.

When the quake ended, Alex slowly relaxed his fingers and pried them from the stone. He put one hand over his heart, which was beating too fast. "That earthquake was terrifying."

"That was *my name*," the rock said, and Alex could sense genuine hurt and disappointment in its voice. The last vestiges of his fear drained away. This was the second time he had hurt its feelings.

It stood up and stumped around the cavern for a few minutes, giving Alex time to think. It was tending to the cavern, as meticulously as someone trimming a bonsai tree. It had one hand on a stalactite, smoothing it, when it said, "Perhaps if you told me your name we could think of something more suitable for you to call me."

Alex smiled and walked over to the creature. He put one hand on its monstrous hand. "My name is Alex. It's not as great as your name, but I like it okay."

The rock smiled—or, rather, the fissure on its face opened and turned slightly upward. "A lovely name. Alex. I should like to have that as a name, too. You may call me Alex."

Alex laughed. "No, I've chosen a name for you already. I promise I won't be afraid anymore."

"Good!" The stone-man bent down low to his face. "What is my new name?"

"I'll call you 'Pookie,'" he said. "There's nothing scary about that."

The rock nodded. "It has a fearsome sound in my own language. But if it pleases you, then my name shall be Pookie. Let us sit again, and I will tell you my story." Pookie cocked his head sideways, as if he was listening to something far away. "The grumbacher is headed to the west, and I think soon enough you will leave. But let us become friends before you go."

Being reminded of the grumbacher made Alex think of Validus. He remembered Apul saying the word when they were talking about Mr. Jurgins, and he assumed that meant he was a monster of some kind. He hoped Val was okay and more than that he hoped to find her again. There wasn't much he could do about either of those things, though, so he resolved to make the best of his situation, and try to enjoy his time in the cave.

"I would like that, Pookie," he said, patting the rocky giant on the arm. "I would like that very much."

Chapter Five

DANGER
ON THE ROAD

It didn't take long for Validus and Benjamin to catch up with Apul. As soon as they were in earshot, he called, "All speed must be made for the Citadel. Our lives and the lives of our loved ones hang in the balance."

Benjamin sat deliberately in the road and began to groom herself, licking her paws. When Apul snorted in annoyance, she said, "The girl can't be expected to keep up with us, Apul." She looked sidelong at Validus. "She only has two feet."

"I could ride on Apul."

Apul stared at her reproachfully, and a toothy grin spread across Benjamin's face.

"He's not like the horses from your world, dear." She looked to the horse. "I can't keep up with you either, Apul."

"You can run fast enough."

"Over short distances. I don't have your stamina." They started to walk along the moons-lit road. Flat but narrow, the road was little more than a worn strip through the plain. The wheat had at last fallen behind them, and the Wide River turned a corner to greet them. Validus couldn't see the far side of the river, though Benjamin said she probably could in the daylight.

Apul snorted. "I won't waste another moment. I'll go ahead and tell old Crackbeak what has happened. You follow at your own pace."

"Stop for a moment and think, Apul. If Validus is the paladin, she is our last hope to stop Silverback and his followers. Your place is with us, to protect her."

"If she is our last hope, then our hope is pinned on nothing. Two experienced paladins were sent out, and neither of them returned. Whether the girl comes to grief on the road now or in the Court of the Breakers later will make little difference."

Validus scuffed her sneakers into the dirt. "I vote for later," she said. "Or, you know, *never* 'coming to grief' would be okay with me too."

Apul trotted a few feet ahead of them and then stopped, his ears perked toward Benjamin expectantly. "If you're waiting for me to say it's okay for you to leave us," Benjamin said, "then you'll still be standing there tomorrow. Get out, if that's what you're going to do."

He flattened his ears against his head and showed his wide, flat teeth. "I'll come back with word from the Citadel." Then he left at an easy trot, quickly picking up the pace until he galloped out of sight.

Benjamin shook her head. "Impatient and foolish," she said. "Old Crackbeak will snap him in two when he gets to the Citadel. If he's not back with us before we cross the Passage of the Winds, then I'll eat my tail."

She turned the green lamps of her eyes up to Validus. "How long can you run?"

Not for long, Validus knew. She had to do twelve-minute runs in gym class, but she didn't like it. By the end she was ready to crawl into a swimming pool so she could cool off and get enough to drink. "Ten or twelve minutes?" Validus said. She shrugged. "If I had to."

Benjamin's eyes widened. "That's not too bad. Let's run a short way."

Validus did her best to keep up with the giant cat, who would run ahead and then stop and wait for her to catch up before leaping off again. After about ten minutes, Val stopped in the middle of the road, panting and resting her hands on her knees. The tiger came back to her and flopped down in the road. "Sit, Paladin. Rest for a moment."

Validus went over to the enormous tiger and leaned against her wide body. She buried her face in her fur, feeling close to her and safe. A deep throbbing sound came from Benjamin's throat. *Purring*, Validus thought, but then she remembered big cats can't purr, only growl. Val's head snapped up. Benjamin rose to her feet, her ears pinned forward, and turned back down the road, the direction from which they had come. "Crawl onto my back," Benjamin whispered. "We must move more quickly."

"What is it?" The hairs on Validus's arms were standing on end, her eyes wide open and her hands digging into Ben's fur. She heard a high, thin voice like the wind whistling through cracks in a chimney.

"Vaaaaaaaaaaaaliduuuuuuuuuus!"

She swung up onto Benjamin's back. "Go," she whispered fiercely.

"Don't fall." With two quick leaps they were on the western road again. Validus heard the voice call her name, but this time she thought she heard recognition, as if it had seen her. She gripped Benjamin's fur, her feet digging into the tiger's haunches. She risked a look backward by laying her head on Benjamin's back and looking under her arm at the road.

The creature stood nearly as tall as a man, pale white with enormous fangs, enormous domelike eyes, and bizarre tentacled limbs. It let loose a triumphant cry and dropped to a prone position, its tentacles propelling it forward across the packed dirt road. Validus twisted around so quickly she lost her grip and slipped to the side, her feet and legs dragging for a second before she lost her grip completely. Benjamin snatched Validus in her teeth and dragged her to her feet. Validus leapt onto Benjamin's back again, but the creature hadn't slowed when Validus fell. It ate up the space between them like a half-starved wolf eating prey. Validus could see its face now—a bloated, disfigured face that looked just like Mr. Jurgins.

She held on with all her might, desperately praying she wouldn't end up on the ground again, mere feet from the grumbacher. Still, a tiger is nearly impossible to ride, especially if it is running. They stretch themselves to their full length with each forward movement, gather their limbs, and shoot forward again. Every time Benjamin hit the ground, Validus shot forward, her head jerking past Benjamin's just as she leapt and yanked her forward again.

Validus's head snapped around like a kite in the jet stream. Her fingers felt as if they would rip into tiny shreds, and her arms ached. One quick look behind her, though, was enough to make her grit her teeth and hold on tighter.

The road was growing steadily higher, moving away from the Wide River. The river dropped below them as the road climbed, and the river meandered through a canyon now. "Take courage, Validus. We're getting close! This is where the river begins to be called the Citadel River." The western road began to twist into the heights, and for brief moments, the grumbacher fell completely out of sight behind them. It hadn't tired or slowed since it gave chase.

Benjamin tore around another corner and told Validus to lean close to her face. "I can't keep this pace," she gasped, "but I have an idea. If you jump into the river from here, maybe the grumbacher will keep after me. It should give you time enough to get to the Passage of the Winds. If the Architect is watching us, maybe Apul will be waiting for us there. He could outpace this grumbacher."

Validus looked over the edge. She didn't know who the Architect was, and the fall from here to the water looked unsafe. "I don't know which way to go."

"Up. At every turn, every choice, move upward, and you will find the Citadel soon enough. Or rather, you will come to the Passage of the Winds. There's no time to discuss it," she said, turning another corner. "That thing could be on us in moments, and it mustn't see you jump."

Benjamin shook Validus from her back. She moved cautiously to the edge of the road, her sneakered toes hanging over the edge. The sun was rising over the plains behind them, and she could see the water below sparkling in the light. *Feet first*, she told herself. *Feet first, and you'll be fine.* "I'll see you at the Citadel," she said, not at all certain this was true.

"At the Passage," Benjamin said, "there is one thing you must know to pass it unharmed—" She stopped in midsentence, and Validus saw her ears perk toward the road. Without another word, she whipped around and ran off, at the same moment that Validus heard the high voice of the grumbacher rise in a keening wail. She looked down again. With a deep breath she stepped over the edge, arms flailing and feet kicking.

Validus wondered for the next several seconds how much hitting the water would hurt, and then she knew exactly how much. The water clapped shut on her head, and she bounced off the sandy bottom of the river. She pushed for the surface, angrily deriding herself for not slipping her shoes off before she jumped. She managed to get her head above water and took a deep breath. She swam painfully to the riverbank at the foot of the cliff and dragged herself out on the rocks.

She lay there a moment trying to catch her breath before she thought to look up at the high pass. What she saw sent her scrambling to her feet.

The grumbacher hung low over the cliff, its deformed Mr. Jurgins head hanging as far over as it could without falling. A moment later it propelled itself off the side, wrapping itself into a ball and splashing hard into the river. Validus leapt onto the wall and started climbing, her hands going out ahead of her, looking for cracks or handholds. She didn't see the grumbacher surface, but she knew the safest thing was to assume it would.

About halfway up the face of the cliff, she found a wide ledge to stretch out on. Her fingernails were cracked, bleeding, and covered in dust, and her arms, legs, and fingers ached. The morning sun was just beginning to warm and dry her. She peered over the lip of the ledge and, to her dismay, saw an inhumanly white shape press itself to the rock face and hiss when she looked down. She wanted to rest. She wanted to be home in a warm bed, sleeping. She wanted Benjamin to tell her what to do. But she had none of those things. So she started climbing again, her heart beating in her chest at the thought of that creature coming up behind her.

Soon she found another, wider ledge, and she thought she could see the road above her, not too far away. She started climbing again, without looking back at the grumbacher. Every moment she paused to decide where to go next, where to make the next reach, she imagined the grumbacher grabbing her ankle with a pale tentacle and tearing her off the rock face, sending her tumbling to the river below.

"Validus," a voice whispered. "I only want to talk to you."

She knew panic could be as dangerous as the grumbacher. The voice of the grumbacher was way too close, but a wrong move could send her hurtling down to break her back on a ledge. She debated jumping back down into the river, but she feared the grumbacher would splash down beside her and she wouldn't be able to get away.

Validus reached up one last time and found to her joy that her entire arm came down on a wide, flat space. A moment's scrambling and pulling and she was back on the road! She laughed out loud and rolled onto her back, enjoying the thought of walking—walking!—the rest of the way to the Citadel.

Giddy with her freedom she stayed for one moment too long on her back. A white tentacle nosed over the edge. Validus scrambled to get away from it, but it struck like a snake and wrapped itself around her thigh. She punched at it and pulled against it as hard as she could, but it dragged her toward the edge.

Validus and the grumbacher fell together to the wide ledge below, Validus landing on top of it. The creature made a sickening sound beneath her, like a snail being crushed. Validus rolled off of it, but it slung itself onto her chest, its pasty white face and oversized fangs only inches from her. "I remember you," it said. "You are the last thing I hunted before being cut to pieces. But why must I find you?" It smacked her head against the stone. "Tell me! Who are you?"

"Validus Smith," she said. She gagged and coughed. "I'm just a kid. There's no reason to hurt me."

It shuddered, and Mr. Jurgins's face trembled like gelatin. When it stopped, the face was clearer. "More memories," it said. "They are coming back to me. Yesssss. Validus Smith. The . . . paladin? Can that be? A child, a simple child? Are you the paladin, Validus Smith?"

Of course not, she thought. *I'm not trained. I'm just a kid. I don't even know what it* means *to be the paladin.* But then there was the voice in the principal's office, the voice that spoke so clearly, that said she *was* the paladin. For some reason that voice seemed a greater argument than any other one that came into her head. And what was a paladin? A hero. She had gathered that much from Benjamin and Apul. A knight, a defender of the worlds, the palace guard of Earth. *The paladin*, she thought, *would not lie on her back listening to a grumbacher whine to itself. A paladin would fight this monster!*

She rolled to the edge, smashing the grumbacher with her full weight, then swung her legs and body over the edge, her fingers barely catching on the rock and keeping her from falling. The grumbacher cried out, startled, and fell. It caught onto her leg with a tentacle, and without hesitation Validus swung her leg forward and back until the grumbacher flew like a pendulum.

Then, with all her might, she kicked the rock wall in front of her. The grumbacher slammed into the rock and dropped, its legs twisting in helpless gyrations until it crashed onto the next ledge down. A menacing growl came from it, and Validus scrambled to her feet so she could start climbing before it could leap for her. The entire ledge the grumbacher was on cracked, broke into a thousand shards, and careened off the mountainside, splashing into the river and taking the grumbacher with it. A shower of rocks followed, hitting the water like shrapnel.

Validus watched the river below, her chest heaving. The grumbacher didn't surface. She turned toward the rock wall and stared at it. She wasn't sure she had the strength to climb again. She sighed and reached out for the stone, but it moved beneath her hands. Startled, she took a half step backward and watched in amazement as the stone face of the cliff collapsed, moved back, and formed a stairway leading up to the road. She thought it might be a trick, but she was too tired to care. She walked stiffly up the stairs until she stood on the road again and the stairs smoothed away into the wall.

Validus turned to the right and started ascending the path, stubbornly putting one foot out, then letting it rest while she dragged the other one forward. She didn't care anymore if the grumbacher was following her. She couldn't go any faster than this.

Hours later, Validus didn't smile or wave when she saw Apul ahead, walking toward her on the road. She focused on keeping awake and moving. She hoped Apul had water, but she didn't say anything. She just put her arms around Apul's neck and dragged herself up onto his back.

"Where's Benjamin?" Apul asked.

But Validus couldn't speak, couldn't think, and soon, couldn't stay conscious.

Chapter Six

POOKIE'S STORY

Humming to himself, Pookie set about making the cave more comfortable for Alex. He made a thronelike chair rise from the ground and used sand to make it soft, almost like cushions. Alex mentioned being a little cold, and his chair immediately heated up. "I piped a little lava in there," Pookie explained shyly.

Alex tucked his legs up under himself, feeling unaccountably sleepy. He yawned and said, "Pookie, you don't have to tell me your story. I trust you now."

"I rarely get visitors. It would be a pleasure to share my story. In fact, you can help me when you get to the Citadel. Those animals have forgotten my story. The castle's foundations tell me many nonsensical rumors it has overheard. So settle into your chair. Yes, that's good. And I will begin."

With an earthshaking jolt, Alex's chair moved. He jumped, but Pookie waved for him to stay in his seat. A dark passageway opened up in the side of the cave, and Alex's chair slid into it, Pookie stomping along behind him. A sort of window suddenly opened in the side of the rock, and natural light flooded into the passage. Alex looked through the window and saw a long plain with distant mountains, the wind tearing across the wide expanse of land.

"Is that Kansas?"

"No. It is a place called Hawk's End, in another world from this one or from your own. Your world, which you call Earth, is connected to eleven more worlds. This is one of them. It is similar to your own from several centuries ago."

In the far distance, Alex could see people riding horses. But then he saw something else, flying above their heads. It seemed small at first, but as it came closer he saw that it was, in fact, a man. He wore a strange bird costume and flew through the sky. "That is the Crimson Hawk," Pookie said. "He rules a large part of his world through the magic given him from another dimension. I am watching him carefully because I am concerned he is an agent of the Blight."

"What is the Blight?"

"I will show you soon." Pookie waved at the wall, and three more windows opened. Through one Alex saw towering skyscrapers and flying cars zipping between the towers. Through another he saw a junglelike landscape, the whole view covered in dense vines and trees and hanging moss. But when Alex leaned closer, he could see some of the plants were shaped like people and were walking around, talking to one another. The last window showed a forest, and the trees and stones and even the rivers all seemed to be talking among themselves.

"These three worlds, and Hawk's End, are four of the healthier worlds connected to your own. They have fought back the Blight, or at least kept it from spreading. The fifth healthy world is the one you just came from. The one with the talking animals."

"Talking *animals*? That's crazy."

"You're talking to a rock right now."

Alex shrugged. "Good point. So, these are healthy worlds. Are there unhealthy ones too?"

"Yes." The chair started moving again, and Alex held onto the armrests as they grated into another room, this one with five windows. The light was paler here, and Pookie's voice dropped in a way that made Alex think he was sad about something. "I had a world like yours, once, that I was the guardian of. But when the Blight came, I did not ask for help. I tried to stop it myself, and over the course of some years it killed all the creatures in my care. They were tiny balls of living light."

The first window opened, and Alex saw a dark landscape with creatures like were-wolves running in a pack along a ridge.

Behind them came an army of pasty, colorless creatures that looked something like insects but with long tentacles instead of legs. "This is a Locked World. We evacuated everyone who desired to leave. The Blight has become too strong on this one, and it will slowly devour all those who remain. Those poor wolf creatures will soon become like their pursuers. They will be Servants of the Blight."

The other four windows opened, and Pookie gestured to each in turn. In the first window, men who looked more like bugs rode on giant dragonflies, battling the creatures of the Blight. "Those are the Insect Lords. They were too proud to leave their world, and now there are only a handful left." He gestured to the next, which looked out on a swamp. Lizards larger than men scurried through the trees, and as they jumped and hid, they changed their shape into other things.

While Alex watched, one jumped down on a Blight creature and tore it to bits. "The doppelgangers. That's what your people have called these lizards. They can take the shape of those around them. In time, they can even take on the nature of another creature. No one else is like them in all the universes I have seen. Many of them left their homes, and they fight against the Blight in many worlds today."

He pointed at another window, which showed a dark tunnel through stone, and a series of short, grim men and women hard at work. "These underground folk have continued to fight so hard I've begun to wonder if your people locked their world too soon." He pointed to the last window, and Alex saw a parade of slow-moving men and women in white robes, singing and moving along in a lengthy line. "The people here are still in denial. They do not acknowledge the Blight, and though it is still weak in their world, we locked them out because it will spread quickly in such an environment."

"So the Blight . . . what? Brainwashes people?"

"It eats them, Alex. It makes them something they are not. And when they are changed into those creatures, their greatest joy is to do the same to others. I must show you one more world." The throne moved again until they were in a small, dark chamber. "This is Dantis, the Dead World. The Blight would be pleased to make all worlds like this one."

The window opened, and Alex looked out on a stark, gray landscape, the only light the harsh stars in the black sky above. "It looks like the moon," Alex said.

"But once it was a lush and thriving world, with gardens and oceans and many fascinating creatures. Now it is as you see it." Pookie was silent for a long time. "The world I once protected would be like this, also, but the creator of the living lights I protected destroyed my planet." Pookie sighed. "I was once a planet myself. When he destroyed me, my heart, that piece of me that we are in now struck another planet with such force that it shattered dimensional boundaries, so

I am now a creature of many worlds. And I have been tasked with helping you and your worlds fight against the Blight, using my own mistakes to guard against your worlds making similar mistakes."

"So the Blight . . . it wants to make Earth like this dead world?"

"Yes."

Alex rearranged himself on his rock throne, taking another sip from the cool water in his goblet.

"So how do you do all these things?" Alex asked. "How do you see where the Blight is spreading? How do you warn people?"

Pookie jumped up and clumped around the chamber, happily humming to himself. He came back with twelve stone balls of various colors, some of them blue with clouded white or deep red or even shades of yellow. "These are the worlds I can see, or, rather, models I have made of them. Here is the world from which you entered my heart, the one with the talking animals."

He handed the ball to Alex. It was cool, smooth, and heavy and colored a brilliant gold. He ran his hands over it and felt a strange soft spot. Turning it in his palm, he found the soft spot. It was black, like ink. "The Blight," Pookie said. "A creature named Silverback has convinced others to help him break into a Locked World. If they succeed—" Pookie paused and looked away for a long time. "But we cannot allow that. We must not dwell on such things."

"Can I see Earth?"

"Hmmmm? Oh! You mean your universe?" Pookie drummed his stone fingers on the table, and it rumbled in reply. "I don't think you would like to see that. It is not an encouraging planet to look at. Still, there are those who stem the tide. Without them, it would be a Locked World already. Look at this instead. You can see your friends and how they are faring."

Alex jumped up and followed him to a corner of the room. Pookie reached into a wall and pulled out a three-dimensional map as if it were a tray. Tiny mountains reached up to them, and a wide river sparkled with sapphires. "Here's me," Pookie said proudly, pointing with his thick fingers. "And, let's see. Ah. Here is your friend, the girl." He pointed to a mountainside.

Alex squinted and strained but couldn't see anything.

Pookie grunted. "One minute, one minute." He pulled out another drawer, which gave a closer look to the same area, and Alex could see Validus, or at least a little model of her made out of jewels and stones, wrestling with a disgusting, tentacled creature. "The grumbacher," Pookie said. "So it caught up with your friends after all. Alex, do you think your friend would survive a fall off that cliff? It seems precarious."

"Maybe," Alex said. "Can we do anything to help her? Can you shoot that grumbacher off with lava or something?"

"Oh dear," said Pookie. "They *are* close to the edge. No, I cannot do anything like that without hurting your friend."

The tiny Validus swung down onto the side of the cliff, smashing the grumbacher into the wall. It dropped onto her leg, and she kicked it into the rocks, hard. It dropped off of her and onto a ledge below.

"Got you!" Pookie said, and he collapsed the grumbacher's ledge, tossing it into the tiny model of the river. With a gleeful laugh he pinched off some more rocks and dropped them into the water after the grumbacher. "That should keep the nasty little creature down for a while. Your friend did well. You didn't tell me she was a paladin. Your paladin is one of the reasons your world hasn't been locked, as well as the fact that the five healthy worlds wish to keep access to the Sword of Six Worlds, which belongs to your paladin. Are you one of the Twelve Peers as well?"

Alex gaped at him and then stared at the tiny Validus, who faced the rock wall with obvious chagrin. "I didn't even know Validus was the paladin until you said so. Are you sure?" He bent down in front of Pookie and formed a small stone stairway in the model, in front of Validus.

"After so many years one can sense these things," said Pookie. "Not everyone throws grumbachers around like that."

When Validus reached the top, Alex smoothed out the stairway with his palm. He wished he could help her more. He watched her walk up the path for a long time.

The long silence finally became obvious to him, and he looked quickly to Pookie. He was staring at Alex and at the map in front of them. "Not everyone can manipulate my maps, either," he said. "You may not be a paladin, but you are something. Something powerful. Come, I think we should get you to the Citadel as quickly as we can. You may be precisely who they need to defeat the Breakers and keep that Locked World locked."

He spread his hands in a wide circular motion, and a tunnel opened up before them. Pookie's tame lights bobbed and flickered on the ceiling. He pointed at four of them, and they raced down the corridor. Pookie took Alex's arm in his wide, stone hand, and they raced after the pools of soft light and toward the Citadel.

Chapter Seven

THE PASSAGE
OF THE WINDS

Validus heard a faraway voice calling her. She thought at first it was her mother waking her for school, but at the same moment, she felt a deep sorrow because she knew her mother wasn't here and she would probably never see her again. Just like Miss Holly, just like Alex and Benjamin and a whole world full of others. Friends she loved, relatives. She would never have her mother feel her forehead in that goofy way she did, announcing her temperature as normal. She wouldn't see her dad with his towers of books, translating some ancient epic.

A jarring impact finally woke her when the voice did not. She rolled her eyes open and found herself dumped onto the parched, dusty rocks. Apul's long face loomed into view. "Get up," he said. "I can't carry you any farther. Each creature must cross the Passage of the Winds on its own four feet." He looked at Validus out of the corner of his eye. "Or two."

Val stretched her arms and legs. Her fingers ached from gripping Apul's mane so tightly, and her limbs protested the movement. The stallion stamped impatiently, sending up a cloud of red dust. "This way," he said and trotted around the corner of the cliff. Validus followed.

The sight on the other side caught Validus unaware and burned into her memory. A wide canyon stretched out toward the horizon, the valley floor thousands of feet below. A narrow network of natural stone bridges snaked into the distance, each bridge wide enough for three people to walk side by side. The thin columns of stone supporting the bridges looked far too tall and thin. They didn't look as if they could hold for long.

Some of the bridges turned over into monstrous roller-coaster loops or corkscrews, but all of them wended their way toward a strange castle. It looked like photographs Validus had seen of termite mounds in Africa—monstrous, smooth, rounded towers filled with holes. The distant structure had thirty or more towers instead of a lone citadel, but the sun hit it in a way that made it shine, and it looked beautiful despite the dangerous path to reach it.

Apul fixed Val with his large brown eyes. "Did Benjamin tell you about the Passage?"

"She mentioned it, but she said she'd be with me when the time came to cross it." Her voice cracked. Benjamin would have been here by now if she hadn't run into trouble.

Apul shook his mane. "Don't talk like that here, Validus. The Passage of the Winds makes the Citadel difficult to attack—we can collapse the bridges from the other side if we need to—but they've also become a liability. Mad winds have taken to guarding the bridges, howling across the canyon and prying reckless travelers from the path. They watch who comes and goes, too, and report back to our enemies."

Validus swallowed hard. She could see colored patches of land far below. They were too high for details of the ground to show. A cloud inched along below them. "These mad winds . . . just blow you off the side?"

"We don't bother looking for the bodies afterward," Apul said.

Validus felt queasy. The thought of walking on the delicate bridges without handrails or sides was bad enough. Imagining evil gusts of winds trying to push her off didn't help. "How do you get past the loops? I can't walk upside down."

"You're speaking in negatives again. 'I can't.' 'It's too dangerous.' 'I'll fall.' Those sorts of thoughts allow the mad winds to pry you loose. As for the loops—we defeated the creatures that made this road a hundred years ago, invaders from another universe. In celebration of our victory, a man called the Architect engineered special qualities for the bridges. The surfaces of the bridges hold onto your feet, but they are powered by the trust of those on the path. So long as you trust the Architect's design, the ground will hold onto your feet, whether you're upside down or buffeted by the strongest winds. You are only in danger when you doubt the design."

"Ha ha haaaaa!" a booming voice called from behind them. "That's nothing but a mockingbird epic—a bunch of nonsense and fluff strung together. Next you'll tell her the builders were like enormous beetles, three times the size of a horse."

"That's right," Apul said. "Poisonous mandibles. Spiked feet to hold them to the paths. Compound eyes letting them see in every direction at once. Of course the Architect altered some of the Citadel's design when we captured it."

"You look too dour and serious to believe colt's tales," laughed the speaker, who looked as fabulous as his rich voice sounded. He was an elephant, as large as any living in

Validus's own world, and his tusks curved low from his face and arced spectacularly toward the sky. Silken cords crisscrossed his wide, gray head and body in dazzling rainbows, attaching him to a large cart full of white, star-shaped flowers the size of a man's head. "No one's fallen from the Passage in three hundred years or more."

Validus turned to Apul. "Is that true?"

Apul blew air through his lips. "It always pays to be cautious, and the winds have grown worse since I was a colt."

The elephant chuckled. "Could be, could be. Name's Granger," he said as he wrapped his trunk around Validus's hand and shook it grandly. He lowered his head toward Val's face and said, "I've tromped farther in a day than most do in their whole lives, but I've never seen anything quite like you. Look a bit like a gorilla, I suppose, if I used my imagination." He cocked his head to one side and blew an exhalation of warm air onto Val's face. He grunted. "If I used my imagination and also squinted."

He let go of Val's hand and flicked his trunk at Apul. "Seen plenty of his sort, of course. They're so scared all the time I recognize them by their tails instead of their faces."

A fourth voice joined the conversation. "That is unkind, Granger, and untrue." An orange and black shape leaped gracefully down the rocks, landing silently behind the merchant pachyderm. Val ran to her and buried her face in her dusty fur. Benjamin nudged Validus affectionately with her head before turning to Granger. "When I agreed to accompany you to the Citadel, it was with the understanding that you would be civil and obedient at all times." She bared her teeth to Apul in a mischievous smile. "He was wandering, lost, on the northern passes."

"Every track leads to a herd," Granger said. "I'm not lost so long as I have customers."

Apul snorted. "This is no time for merchants in the Citadel. But if my striped friend gave her word, then you can travel with us. Remember, though, who the experienced travelers are in this particular passage."

"Oh, I'm quite certain that must be you," the elephant said, rolling his eyes. "No idea why I'd follow a tiger and a horse anywhere. Bound for trouble. My old Mam always said, 'Bound for trouble, that one.' Can't say but she was right, traveling with a colt and a tigress."

"We shall see," Benjamin said. Her tail flicked back and forth like a metronome. "Did you tell Validus about the Passage?"

"Yes," Validus said. "Remember your feet will stay on the path. The Architect's magic is powered by our confidence, so stay convinced that the path can keep the winds from blowing you off. Be positive."

Benjamin laughed, lowering her head and looking at Apul's dour face with her green eyes. "Did he really say that? 'Be positive'? The whole Citadel will buzz with it."

Apul snorted. "Enough. Silverback and his Breakers work night and day to enter the Locked World. Every wasted moment speeds us to destruction."

Granger opened his mouth to speak, but Benjamin was too quick. "He is right. The time has come." She leapt down the path and then turned her agile body to see that they all followed. Apul trotted past her onto the stone bridge. Validus swallowed hard and followed. Benjamin walked alongside her and allowed her to grasp her fur. Granger brought up the rear, his wagon moaning and creaking. The elephant hummed to himself as he walked. Validus feared the bridge wouldn't hold their weight, but it showed no signs of buckling or weakness.

They walked for hours. The winds hadn't bothered them, but Validus still felt queasy anytime she took her eyes off the Citadel. To keep her mind off the journey, she told Ben the story of her encounter with the grumbacher as they walked. As they got closer, the sun shining off the Citadel's white towers was a heartening reminder that this fearful path had an end, eventually, and she noticed it had multicolored flags on many of the towers. There was no wind over there, apparently, because the flags weren't fluttering. She looked once over the edge and immediately regretted it. Benjamin gently asked her to release her fur and walk. Validus had torn a large clump of it from her and was staring over the side, imagining herself falling.

The winds came just as they reached the first of the loops. Validus shivered when the first gust hit, but her feet held firm. "An intimidation technique," Benjamin said. "Be strong. They are trying to frighten you."

"It's only a little gust," Granger said, and his voice boomed out over the wind. "It couldn't lift a grain of sand from this bridge."

Apul went first, to reinforce that the loop was nothing to fear. The wind picked up, and his mane and tail blew toward the edge. He walked up the loop and then continued up the steepness of it with no visible increase of effort. When he reached the top he stayed there for a minute, upside down, before descending to the other side.

The wind grew fiercer. Validus could barely stand. Then the whispers started, and they were more terrible than the height, the wind, or the bridge. *You will fall*, they said. *These creatures have brought you here to kill you. What are you doing here? You should be in your own world, safe. With your parents. You are a child. What right do they have to ask you to do these things? They are too difficult. Turn back.*

Validus felt her feet starting to lift from the ground. Whatever power made her stick and kept her from falling had weakened. She leaned into the wind, but it pushed her along the path, moving her toward the edge. She tried to dig her sneakers into the rock, but they still slid forward.

"Benjamin," she said, starting to panic, but Benjamin was with Granger, trying to calm him down. The elephant was panicking, too. The tarp covering the merchant's flowers whipped loose and flew over the valley like a kite before crumpling in on itself and diving out of sight.

"The bridge will hold," Benjamin said, her voice carrying over the wind. "Be confident." Granger wrapped his trunk around Benjamin's foreleg, and his breathing calmed. The wind lessened then stopped altogether. One last whisper came to her before fading away: *When you are upside down on the loop, we will take you with us, far from this bridge, to the deep down, the far below. Walk to the loop at your peril.*

The wind stopped completely, and Validus almost fell from the sudden lack of resistance. Benjamin rubbed against her side and told her she had done well. Apul waited impatiently at the far foot of the loop. Granger wouldn't meet her eyes.

"The whispers said they would knock me off if I tried to cross the loop."

"Those were mad winds speaking," Apul said. "Don't listen to them." He walked confidently to the loop again, which, at first, was little more than a steep hill. Then it became a wall. And then, of course, a ceiling. Apul stopped at the top, his mane hanging straight down. He lifted his feet one after another. "There is nothing to fear."

Benjamin's green eyes hadn't moved from Val's face. "I will walk behind you," she said. "And Granger behind me. I will not let you fall." When Validus didn't move she said, "Your world is in danger. Your parents and friends. Will you let fear stop you? Be bold and remember the paladin is a being of power. You already defeated the grumbacher."

Validus took a deep breath. The first few steps weren't hard, but when the wall of the loop became the floor, she experienced a moment of vertigo. It didn't hurt, and she continued to stand straight up—or, as it happened to be, straight out. Benjamin gently reminded her to walk, and she moved quickly to the apex of the loop, where she stood defiant of gravity, upside down, her hair the only part of her body continuing to obey gravity.

The last fourth of the loop proved to be the most difficult, as Validus now discovered, because she was facing the clouded view of the distant ground. She bit her lip, but she remembered to move forward. She closed her eyes and took one step at a time. She felt along the path with her feet and edged farther along.

Her foot caught on an uneven place in the path, and her stomach lurched. The sudden sensation of gravity pulling her downward popped her eyes open just in time to see her worst nightmare coming true. She fell, screaming, and a brutal landing on the land bridge cut her scream short, the air forced from her lungs. Her hands shot out and grasped the stone, or tried to. She squeezed her eyes shut, panting. She wouldn't move from this place, not ever.

Warm breath came to her ear. "You tripped, Validus, that is all. You were never close to falling farther than your feet. Stand up."

The wind was blowing again. *You are too clumsy to go on without killing yourself,* the winds said. *You can't save the world if you're dead.* "I can't," Validus said, her eyes still shut. "I'll fall."

Apul's horsy breath came to her just before he grabbed hold of her shirt and dragged her along the loop until they came to the wider expanse of the bridge. Apul said something, but Validus could only hear the wind now. She knew she would never make it to the other side of the bridge alive.

Validus thought it useless to resist, insane to attempt to stop the machinations of Silverback, who was a servant of the great Blight, a force that could not even be isolated to confront. And the silver blade of the Paladins, the Sword of Six Worlds, had already been broken, its pieces set on a pedestal near Silverback's mine. Every day he stood in front of the sword and mocked the Paladins, the Architect, and the Twelve Peers. The former paladin of Earth watched, still living, held captive by a silver chain. A paladin from another world was dead. He tried to kill Silverback but could not. In his world he was paladin for twenty years, trained by a great and powerful paladin of a neighboring world. He rode into battle many times. How could she, a child, untrained, hope to succeed where he failed?

"You are speaking of things you cannot know," Apul said to Validus, gently. Only then did she realize what she had been muttering, and only then that she was speaking aloud.

"The winds," Granger said. Then, to Apul: "I did wrong to doubt you. These mad winds are indeed a trouble to little creatures, though I have no fear of them. Perhaps if I carried her on my back. Or in my cart."

"Yes!" Validus shouted. She couldn't walk any longer. The thought of moving along that endless bridge filled her with terror. She imagined herself in Granger's wagon, lying in a perfumed bed of flowers and watching the clouds overhead. She could no longer picture what it meant to walk, to trudge along in fear.

"It is not wise to lift her feet from the path," Benjamin said.

"She must walk," Apul said. "She is in greater danger of being pried loose by the winds if you carry her, and I have never seen them speak so clearly to someone. They are breathing their lies into her ears."

"Nonsense," said Granger. "The paladin cannot walk. I will carry her. She is small and helpless."

"Now the winds speak through you! And it was ill spoken when you called her paladin. The winds carry your words to Silverback even now!"

"Peace," Benjamin said, her voice calm even as the winds whipped up to a greater magnitude, nearly carrying away her words. "I called her paladin myself only a few moments ago. Validus must make her own choices in this matter."

"She's untrained!" Apul shouted.

"The Architect chooses the paladin, and he is at least three centuries old! Who are we to argue with his choice?"

"We're not certain she was chosen," Apul said.

Validus cut the argument short. "I'll ride with Granger. I'm too afraid to walk anymore."

Without another word Granger scooped Validus up with his trunk and helped her climb onto his broad gray back. She lay on her stomach, arms stretched as far as she was able around the elephant's thick neck, and they began to trudge forward against the wind. Validus could feel Granger's voice vibrating. She couldn't hear the words, but Granger continued his long soliloquy for the next hour.

The wind died down for short periods, but it seemed that the moment Validus loosened her grip on the elephant, the wind would howl back across the bridge. More than once Validus wondered if her position on Granger's back was more dangerous than walking—it seemed the winds had a better grip on her here. Still, the thought of any downward movement at all paralyzed her.

After a while, Validus noticed how close they were to the far side, and her spirits began to rise. Only a few more curving strokes of bridge and they would be on the Citadel road. A rabbit startled from behind a small rock and sped up toward the castle. "It's Baruth!" shouted Apul. "Tell them we're coming home!" The rabbit ran so quickly it crossed what remained of the bridge in less than two minutes. Validus watched the rabbit until his feet hit the wide Citadel road. Benjamin let loose a contented sigh.

"We always breathe easier after the sentinel," she said.

"I can't wait to get past this canyon. I'm sure Granger will be glad to get me off his back." Granger didn't reply, so Validus leaned over Granger's back and tried to make out the words he had been repeating over and over for some time now. She strained to hear them more clearly.

"Never sell starflowers here anyway with the horse telling everyone I never listen and the Citadel and all their rules and who wants them anyway and here I come carrying it all the way from the great trees, from the great trees! But what do they care? I should leave the whole lot and take them to Lord Silverback, now there's an appreciative one, he would give me whatever I asked for this load and never say a word. Here at the Citadel though, I'll never sell starflowers—." He went on this way for some time.

Validus tried to talk to him, but he wouldn't reply. She debated telling Benjamin, but Apul had just crossed off the bridge and Validus didn't want to do anything that would slow their exit from the precarious place over the canyon.

A gust of wind came suddenly and struck Validus like a fist. She fell off Granger's back, barely managing to tangle one arm into the complicated cords tied onto the elephant. She took one dizzying swing over the canyon and landed with a thud against Granger's broad side. She tried to scramble back up, but the wind came again, steadier now, and Val felt herself pushed away from the elephant. She held onto the cords, and the wind carried her farther out, over the side of the bridge like a kite.

Validus screamed and started to reel herself in, pulling hand over hand down the cords, when, to her horror, the peddler's cart lifted from the bridge and swung over the side. Granger strained to move forward, to make it to the far side of the bridge, but the airborne cart worked against him. Validus could feel Granger losing his solid footing. Benjamin sprang into action, ripping and tearing at cords with teeth and claws. The cart tore loose from Granger and spun off the bridge, but Granger reached out with his trunk and tangled it into the main cord lines.

"Granger, you fool, let it go!"

"My starflowers! You just want them for yourself!"

"You'll go with them if you don't let go!" It was true. Granger's feet were sliding toward the edge, the cart acting as a monstrous sail. Validus saw in an instant that she would go over the edge with Granger unless she could get onto the ground. The voices in the wind spoke to her again, but she ignored them, wrapped one hand up in the cords, and then reached for another, lower cord to work herself down toward the bridge. Granger's rear feet were off the ground now, kicking, his massive front feet stamping and scrabbling for a hold.

"Let the cart go!" Validus yelled. "You'll kill us both!" But Granger only rolled his head and leaned forward, trying to keep his feet on the bridge. Another four cords down and Validus would be able to reach safety, but she doubted that Granger would last that long. Should she jump for it? She imagined leaping for safety only to be picked up by one of the mad winds. Better to crawl down the ropes. She followed the ropes down, and now she was up against the elephant's side. A giant gust nearly tore her from her hand-hold, and Granger slid inevitably for the edge, his third leg lifting and then his last great round foot barely holding to the bridge for a final heart-racing second before it, too, gave way and the elephant lifted into the air after the cart, Validus clutching to his side.

Benjamin leapt for them, her shiny claws piercing Granger's legs. He let loose a terrible trumpeting cry and began to writhe and kick at Benjamin, who struggled not to lose her grip. Validus lost a handhold, and her legs flew out like a flag snapping in the wind. Piercing pain raced up her other arm as the wind tried to yank her free from the cords. "Quickly!" Benjamin said, her lips pulled back to show her sharpened teeth. "I can't hold him."

Two eternal seconds passed before Apul warily came close enough to the struggling elephant that Validus could wrap her hand into Apul's mane and jump. A last violent gust blasted them, and Apul whickered in pain as Val used his mane to keep from falling and then slid to the ground, a sudden firmness greeting the soles of her shoes. She couldn't fall if she kept her feet on the bridge, she reminded herself, and it felt as if the bridge took a firmer hold on her feet. The winds seemed to realize this, too, and the moment her feet hit the ground the winds died all around her. Granger, however, landed a vicious blow on Benjamin's face, knocking her to the ground. He lifted in slow motion, like an overloaded helicopter, and spun slowly away from them. He dipped slightly about ten feet out, and then the winds howled around him and, instead of falling, he rapidly gained altitude. Validus stared after him, numb, until Granger was little more than a rotating gray blur in the distance.

Benjamin nudged Val's hand gently with her head. "You can't save him now, Validus."

"The mad winds were talking to him. He kept mumbling about not being able to sell his flowers at the Citadel. I should have known."

"It is difficult to know when the mad winds speak to your own heart. To know when they are speaking to another requires great discernment."

Validus absently scratched Benjamin's head, happy to have a friend nearby who didn't blame her for what had happened to Granger. She stepped from the bridge onto solid ground, but all sense of victory or relief was gone. She only felt sorrow for Granger. Even as the Citadel towered above her, a majestic testimony to the work of paladins past, she couldn't think of victory or even survival. She kept seeing Granger lifting into the air. She wondered where Alex was and whether he was safe. Then they passed through the narrow gate into the Citadel, and her first day as paladin—if she really was a paladin—began in earnest.

Chapter Eight

THE CITADEL

The gate looked low and narrow when seen in the context of the towering Citadel. Smooth, white towers slid up into the sky, but Validus couldn't tell what it was made from. As they passed through one enormous gate, she touched the stone and it was cool as marble.

As soon as they passed the gate, Apul bolted off into the crowd of animals that crisscrossed up and down the busy walkways and tunnels of the Citadel. Benjamin called after him, but he didn't respond. She huffed, then nudged Validus toward a central podium jutting from the traffic.

A rhinoceros jostled Validus as it lumbered by. "Sorry, sorry," it said. "I'm not designed for tight places." Then it swirled on in the raucous river of flamingos, giraffes, horses, house cats, mice, and penguins, bumping into hippos and accidentally knocking down a brown bear who stood on his hind legs to get a better view over the crowd. "Sorry," she heard it call. "Not exactly the savannah in here." Then the river swallowed it, and Validus couldn't see it any longer.

Benjamin tugged on her sleeve. "I have some business before the Council meets," she said. "I will leave you in Yorrick's capable claws." She nodded toward an armadillo who balanced awkwardly atop the central podium, a long scroll spilling from one scaly claw, his other clutching a tiny silver monocle to his eye. A small rat perched contentedly beside him, combing its whiskers.

"What's that? Who said my name?" the armadillo cried, and the monocle dropped and rolled off the side of the podium, hitting the ground with a distant ting of metal striking stone. "Drat!" He scrambled after the monocle and lost his grip on the scroll, which slid off the other side. He looked over his rounded shoulder just in time to see the last bit of paper slip over the edge. He let loose an unintelligible cry and slid across the pedestal, tiny claws straining toward the scroll, but he overshot and went over the side himself. In an act of amazing agility he spun in midair and grasped the lip of the pedestal, scurrying with his hind legs until he made it to the top once again. He twirled to look over the side at the fallen scroll, and his tail knocked the contented rat in the chest, sending him flailing from the pedestal to the ground, a look of profound surprise on his face.

The armadillo settled his monocle onto his needle nose, giving him an enormously magnified right eye. He twiddled his claws together in a nervous gesture, then motioned for the rat to climb back up with the scroll. Just as the rat reached the top, Benjamin cleared her throat and said, "Yorrick." The armadillo was so startled he knocked the poor rat to the ground again. The rat squeaked his displeasure and then lay on the ground, wrapped in the scroll like a toga. The armadillo slowly peeled his fingers from his eyes and peered out at Benjamin. "Ah," he said. "You must learn not to use someone's name without warning him."

Benjamin chuckled, and Validus couldn't help herself. She burst into laughter, startling the poor armadillo even further. "How would I get your attention, Yorrick, without using your name?" Benjamin asked. "You don't like people to tap you because it startles you. If we sit in a corner and wait to be noticed, it frightens you. Do you have a suggestion on how we could get your attention?"

"Certainly," Yorrick said, pulling a small pair of spectacles from his tiny red vest. A moment of confusion followed when he placed them over his monocle, but he soon recognized the problem, pocketed the monocle, and settled the spectacles onto his pointed snout. He looked over the rims at Benjamin. "Perhaps the best thing would be to say *someone else's* name. Then I, hearing your voice, would turn and exclaim joyfully that you, my good friend, had returned."

"And I would thank you for your heartfelt welcome, Yorrick," Benjamin said. "Now, I have some complaints for you. The information you provided for our journey was terrible. Our names didn't sound remotely like the natives'."

Yorrick harrumphed. "Ambassador Pierce was not available to help with the names for his homeworld, so I looked those up myself. There were even pictures. Bengal Tiger is a perfectly respectable name for someone with your background."

Validus had barely gained control of herself, but she tried to keep the laughter in this time. She started speaking with a broad smile, and by the time she was done she couldn't speak. The words were washed away in laughter. "I get it now. Benjamin Gultiger! Ha ha ha! She's—" Her sides hurt.

Her mouth ached. She couldn't go on. The thought of Apul's name made her laugh even harder.

Benjamin's lips curled up into a satisfied feline smile, but Yorrick didn't know what to make of the laughing creature before him. He flicked imaginary lint from his jacket, then asked Benjamin how he could help her. Validus tried to pull it together because she could barely breathe. She let loose a deep, joyous sigh. The storm of laughter had passed.

"I have things to do," Benjamin said to Yorrick. "I need to warn the Guardsmen a grumbacher is on our trail. And I need to speak to the rest of the Council." Yorrick's eyes widened. "I have more complaints for you later, but for now can you help Validus get settled? Give her a meal and a place to rest and wash."

"Of course," Yorrick said, and as soon as he nodded Benjamin loped off the way Apul had come, and without a word to Val.

The armadillo looked over at Validus. "Tell me the truth. Have you ever met anyone named Bengal Tiger in your world?"

Validus stifled a laugh. "No, never." The armadillo's face fell. Validus felt so bad that she quickly added, "But Ben is a common name."

"Aha! I knew it!" Yorrick twirled about as if looking for something. "Mannin write that down! Mannin? Mannin! Where is that rat?" He clucked his tongue disapprovingly at the unfurled mess that had been his scroll. The rat was gone. "Always skulking away somewhere. Ah, well. Tell me then, Validus, is it? If I am to make you comfortable, what sort of animal are you?" He pulled a quill from his vest and a tiny pad of paper.

"I'm not an animal, exactly."

Yorrick's eyes lit up. "A vegetable, then? We have some lovely vegetable habitats that haven't been used since my grandmother's time."

"No."

Yorrick looked disappointed but quickly smiled to cover it. "Mineral?"

"No."

He looked perplexed for a moment, but then his face brightened. "An elemental, oh I see. Do you prefer fire, water, air, or earth because we have some lovely water rooms now. We used to have some ether rooms, but I'm afraid we ended up using them as storage closets. It's been so long since an ether-elemental came through here that I wonder if they exist at all. There are fewer elementals overall in the last hundred years. We have a spectacular fire·room. A few salamanders are in there now, but we could move them out since you have come so far."

Validus smiled. "If those are the choices, then I guess I'm an animal, after all."

Yorrick swirled his quill up in the air in triumph, his sharp gray nose quivering in excitement. "I suspected it all along. Wait, don't tell me. I will study you intently." He bit the nub of his quill. "Perhaps you are . . . a pig?"

Validus laughed. "No! I guess I would be closest to an ape or a gorilla."

Yorrick burst into wild laughter. "Outworlders always have the zaniest humor. A gorilla! Ha ha ha! And you with almost no hair! And that little squashed face and the needle snout! Next you'll tell me you're closely related to the dolphins! Ah ha ha haaaaa! Or maybe you're a— Ha ha! Oh I can't even say it. Maybe you're a *frog*. Yes, yes, I can see the resemblance. Ha ha ha! A frog with *ears*!" The armadillo wiped helplessly at the tears rolling down his face. "Sorry," Yorrick said. Another giggle snuck out. "Now I see why you laughed so heartily earlier. With a humor like yours every interaction must be filled with hilarity." He giggled once more, then looked seriously into Val's eyes. "Miss Validus, please tell me what sort of animal you are. A great deal of work is to be done, and of course all our hopes are pinned on the paladin who 'Bengal Tiger' brought back from your world."

Validus shrugged. "I hope people don't get their hopes up too much over this paladin."

The armadillo clucked his tongue. "Perhaps you don't understand. The paladins from your world are particularly respected because of the Sword of Six Worlds. Most paladins try only to protect their own world, but centuries ago the paladin of Earth brought that sword and pledged to protect every world yours touched. Amazing, really, don't you think?"

Validus leaned against the podium. "What makes the sword so great, anyway?"

"Ha ha! Well, I suppose you could ask your mother. Is she the paladin? Oh, I can see from your face that's not right. Perhaps your father or an older sibling then. The sword has shown different powers with different paladins. Some say reflecting the personality of the paladin, and some say reflecting the need of the time. No matter. If your paladin cannot save us from the Blight, then the worlds around us will fall as well. I cannot bear to think of the consequences for us if that were to happen. No, we mustn't even consider defeat, for soon your loved one will leap into courageous battle against all the forces of the Blight! Now, let us make you comfortable before the epic battle begins."

Validus took a step backward. All the worlds were relying on the paladin and she was the paladin, right? Of course Yorrick didn't realize Validus was the paladin because she was a child. The paladin should be older, experienced, aware of the situation. She barely understood where she was, and they wanted her to be their savior. She couldn't even deal with Jeremy, the bully, at school. She barely escaped the grumbacher. Now she was supposed to save the world? And not just one world but multiple worlds! She thought, at least, there would be someone here to help her. She wanted to explain to someone how ridiculous it was to expect her to save the worlds, paladin or not. She put her hand over the armadillo's paw. "Yorrick, I'm just a kid. I don't belong here."

"Of course," Yorrick said, slapping his scaly forehead with the back of his tiny claw. "A goat. I see it now. No horns, but the younger kids don't always show them. You're a hairless variety, aren't you? Well then, let me call a goat to take you up to Blaggard's Rock. Oh! There's Randull now! Randull!"

A small gray and black spotted goat peeled himself out of the river of animals passing Yorrick's podium. He balanced onto his rear feet and placed his front hooves onto the flat space the armadillo sat on. "What is it?"

Yorrick sputtered. "Don't you know how rude it is to put your hooves on my pedestal, Randull?"

Randull rolled his yellow and black eyes into his head and let out a derisive bleat. "So you called me over for etiquette lessons. Bleah!"

"Ignorant and uncouth goat! I called you over so you could take this young kid up to Blaggard's Rock. Give her the best room you have." He pointed his quill at Randull's nose, and flecks of ink sprayed the goat's face. "I'll know if you disobey me, Randull, and I'll have you and your whole crew reassigned to the sea lion rooms."

Randull turned his flat gaze on Validus, and then he looked back at Yorrick. "If that thing is a goat of any variety, then I'm an eagle."

"Fine. You're an eagle. Now scurry along and treat our guest well. She's related to the paladin."

Randull sighed. Yorrick waved cheerily at Validus, but Mannin had just run up bustling with news about more visitors arriving in the top levels. A whole tribe of clouds! The next best thing to water elementals! Could they use the waterfall rooms? Yorrick gathered his scrolls and pen and hurried off after the rat, both of them barely able to conceal their joy as they raced through the tromping feet of the animals.

"Come along then," said Randull wearily. "Let's get you a cold, rocky ledge to sleep on." The goat stepped into the flow of animal traffic around them. Validus hesitated for a minute and then stepped in behind him.

Chapter Nine

THE KING
OF BLAGGARD'S
ROCK

Randull the goat gave Validus a sidelong glance as they moved through the crowd of animals. "Some goat you are. No hair. No horns. Your face is too wide, and you walk on your hind feet. Oh, my cud! What's wrong with your hooves?" Randull moved over to the side of the road and started gagging himself, dry heaves preventing him from talking until he finally gasped out, "It's horrible."

Validus looked down at her feet but only saw her sneakers. She couldn't see why that would be so disturbing, and she said so.

"No," said Randull, gasping. "Your fore-legs. They're deformed. They're split and broken and GAH! Don't move them around like that. I'm going to be sick."

Validus flexed her fingers again and laughed. "Don't worry, it doesn't hurt," she said, and Randull closed his eyes again, his fat sides moving in and out. "I'll put them in my pockets." She shoved her hands into the front of her jeans.

Randull straightened up after a long moment and rolled his long, red tongue out as if stretching it, his eyes squeezed shut. "No wonder you walk on your hind legs. Listen, keep those things out of sight. No reason to get everyone thinking about deformities and torture when the battle against the Blight is so close." He shook his horned head again and made noises like a ninety-year-old man getting into a cold swimming pool. "It could be worse," he said at last. "We're all used to Yorrick by now. Last spring he misheard some stoats and sent them to live with us too.

We can put up with a hairless, split-hooved biped for one night."

"Thanks. I guess."

Randull trotted down a narrow passageway to their left, his tail flicking. "Pick up the pace, two legs." He stopped and regarded Val with his yellow, unblinking eyes. "Blaggard's Rock is the most comfortable place in the whole Citadel. You'll have the best view, a cold, high ledge of rock to sleep on, and plenty of bushes to snack on. You're lucky Yorrick thought you were a goat."

The corridor curved upward, and white sunlight framed an opening ahead of them. The unmistakable tang of ocean air wafted to them, cool and crisp. Validus followed Yorrick through the doorway and out to the base of a jagged peak, jutting incongruously from a calm, smooth beach. The tunnel behind them stuck out of the sand like a great slab of granite. Validus didn't understand how they could be at sea level since the Citadel soared on mountain peaks, approachable only by way of the high and winding Passage of the Winds.

"Blaggard's Rock," Randull said proudly. "Named for my own grandsire's grandsire, Black Guard, who found the passage and claimed this little corner of the Citadel for the goats, during the great war against the Insect Lords. It's a pocket universe, only ten miles square. And it's all ours. Come on then, kid. I'll take you to one of the guest ledges." Randull leapt onto a low, thin shelf of rock, then up to another. Validus scrambled after him but already saw that this might be a daunting task. The rock was jagged and wet with sea spray.

"Maybe I should just sleep on the beach tonight." It couldn't be much colder than sleeping on the rock. If she got too cold, she could slip into the tunnel for shelter from the wind.

Randull bleated. "That would be an insult to our hospitality. Why sleep on the soft, warm beach when we have a cold sliver of rock for you? Why, some of the guest ledges will let you hang your head right over the ocean while you sleep!" His horned head peeked over a ledge up above. "Those lame hooves really slow your climbing, don't they? We're almost to the plain. You can rest there."

It took Validus twenty minutes to climb the rest of the way, and she nearly fell twice. Her arms hurt, her shins were bruised, and she had scrapes on her chin and elbows. She pulled herself up onto a wide, mostly level shelf of rock about the size of a football field.

A variety of goats mulled around, munching on stunted brown shrubs. A monstrous gray goat caught sight of her from across the field and started running straight for her, horns down. Validus looked around frantically for Randull but didn't see him.

The other goat was bearing down on her. She took a few steps sideways, in case it wasn't coming for her, but the goat corrected and poured on speed. Validus crouched, ready to jump to the side at the last moment, wondering if it was going to work. If the goat connected and she went over the side, it would be the end of the road.

Randull streaked up from the side and crashed heads with the gray goat, knocking him far off course and away from Validus. The gray goat gathered itself for another charge, but a small group of goats quietly gathered around him. "What are you thinking, Burgess?" Randull asked. "This kid is our guest. She's related to the paladin from Earth."

"She could be a spy," Burgess said.

Randull snorted. "She's not smart enough." Validus shot him a dirty look, but Randull didn't notice. "I know you're the butt-heads-first-and-ask-questions-later type, Burgess, but that was extreme."

Burgess looked over his shoulder at some of the other goats. More made their way over until two large crowds formed, some behind Burgess and some around Validus. "The Blight is tricky," Burgess said. "How do we know this thing is with the paladin? Look at it, it's all deformed. Look at its hooves."

A collective gasp came from the goats, and Validus shoved her hands into her pockets.

Randull glared at Validus and said under his breath, "I told you to keep those things out of sight." Then to the others he said, "Okay. She's disgusting. Just looking at her makes my stomachs hurt. But she's related to the paladin, and she's our guest. If you don't like it, you can go sleep with the pigs on level four."

Burgess moved closer to Validus, so close she could feel his warm breath as he spit out his words. "How do we know she's not working for the Blight? I say she could be one of Silverback's creatures, and we wouldn't know it. I say she could be here to take out the goats before the big battle because Silverback's afraid of us. We can't trust her. Could be she's sneaking herself in to clip our horns when we're not looking."

Randull stamped his forepaw against the rock. His nostrils flared. "She's just a kid, Burgess. She's got no horns and crippled hooves. We can't know for sure if someone's working with the Blight, that's true. But even if she were, what could this kid do to us? You think she'd survive a fight with any of us?"

Burgess let loose a long bray. "Let's find out. I invoke the rule of Blaggard's Rock. I challenge her to proof by combat." A gasp rose from the assembled goats.

Validus slapped her hand to her forehead. Of course. Now she had to fight a goat to win the right to sleep on a narrow, wet shelf of rock. All the goats ran into the center of the field and made a great clump as they chattered excitedly about the challenge.

Randull nudged Val over to the side of the cliff, and Val bent to hear him. "Okay, kid. This is just a ritual. A couple good knocks to the head, and he's going to let you walk. Hit him harder than usual, though, right? Teach him a lesson for messing with you."

Validus stared at Randull, trying to figure out if he was serious. She tried to speak, stuttered, and then stopped. She pointed to the missing horns that were not on her head. "Do you really think I am going to survive even one hit from that goat? I think it would be smarter to get me back down the mountain."

"No!" Randull glanced back to see if anyone else had heard. "Listen, that would be the same as admitting Burgess is right. The goats will chase you down and kill you if they think you are a servant of the Blight. The only way out of this is to ram the stuffing out of him."

"So I'm going to get killed either way."

Randull scratched at the ground with his feet. He turned his flat gaze back at the goats gathered on the field. "Stay here," he said gruffly. He trotted off to the goats. A great cacophony of bleats and grunts rose a moment later. Validus had the distinct impression they were unhappy sounds. Randull trotted back. "I offered to take your place."

A flood of relief washed over Validus. She might actually live! Long enough to die fighting the Blight, anyway. "Thank you, Randull! I'm sure you can beat him."

Randull snorted. "Any goat with half a horn could beat that old bag of socks. They refused the switch." Validus deflated. She looked over the cliff and wondered which was worse—getting knocked off the side or beaten to death by a goat. "But I convinced them to change the challenge. See that rock over there?" A spine of rock shot up on the far side of the mountain, thin as a needle, jagged and dangerous. The top was flat, and the highest point on Blaggard's Rock. "That's Old Black Guard's Shelf. The kids use the climb as a dare. If you can get to the top before Burgess, he'll leave you alone. And he's willing to give you a head start. He won't go up until you're halfway."

Great. A sudden, relatively quick death was just replaced with a long climb, suffering, and aching muscles and joints, all followed by a quick death. Validus knew there was no way she could beat the goat to the top. Impossible. "What happens if he gets there first?"

"He decides that. He's acting strange. Keeps saying you're an agent of the Blight, and we should kill you or at least maim you in some way. I've never seen him like this."

"Why would anyone serve the Blight?" Validus asked. "If I understand it right, the Blight wants to suck all life out of the planet and leave it an empty husk. Who would want that?"

"Sometimes people want the power to control life more than they want life itself," Randull said. "The Blight makes extravagant promises to its servants."

A pair of scruffy-looking goats came over and nudged at Validus's legs. "Time to get moving for the contest," one of them said. Randull butted one, hard, and sent it mewling away. He gave the other a granite stare, and it shuffled off nervously.

Randull continued giving the two menacing looks until they were back with the group on the plain. He waited for about two seconds and then started over in their direction.

Validus took three quick steps to catch up. Fine. She would die here climbing a cliff, she would die because she fought an ape, or she would die because a grumbacher mauled her. She shouldn't be here—shouldn't be the paladin—and she shouldn't be the one trying to save the world. But she was going to do her best. "Any advice about rock climbing?"

Randull looked at Validus carefully, still trotting toward the assembly of goats ahead of him. "Never take all your hooves off the rock at one time."

It wasn't the best advice Validus had ever heard. She already understood the concept of gravity, maybe a little too clearly after the episode at the Passage of the Winds. But at least it gave her something to laugh about if she fell off the rock. She would have maybe four seconds to think, *Aha! Shouldn't have let go of the rock. I should have listened to old Randull a little more carefully. He is, after all, a mountain goat.* And then she would be dead. But at least she would be smiling.

About thirty goats gathered in a circle around Burgess. Randull nudged Validus into the center. A goat so old his white fur seemed yellow called the others to attention. He nodded to Burgess and then to Validus. "Declare your challenge," the goat said.

Burgess cleared his throat and said, "I challenge this so-called goat to prove her allegiance to the Citadel by a contest of climbing. If I reach the top first, I will pass judgment on her because she is a servant of the Blight. If she reaches the top first, then she may pass judgment on me for passionately defending my people. Since her forehooves are grotesquely mutilated, I will allow her a half-climb start."

A wave of ecstatic head-butts burst out among the younger goats. Randull rolled his eyes at them in a terrible, slow circuit, and they quieted. He turned back to Validus and started chewing his cud, which gave him a strangely vacant expression. The old goat turned wearily to Validus. "Have you, the challenged, any reply?"

Validus scanned the assembled crew of scruffy animals at her knees, spread out around her like bushes with old carpets thrown over them. She couldn't think of a single thing to say. It seemed a shame to remain silent because they might be her last words, but she could feel the weight of the goats' stares in front of her and the weight of the jagged spire of rock behind her. She shrugged. She waved a hand to the old goat to show she had nothing to say, and a disgusted groan rose from the goats. They had seen her poor split hooves again. "Climb," the old goat said.

The first few ledges weren't too bad, and Validus took them like steps. But then she wasn't sure where to go. One narrow edge jutted out to her left, but it was so high she would have to hang from it and pull herself up. She wasn't sure she could balance herself well enough to pull up to standing on the ledge. Her hands started to sweat just thinking about it. The goats were laughing and joking. Her heart pounded and moved up in her chest. Her thoughts came in a jumbled, confused mess until she finally decided she should jump and take her chances. Two deep breaths and she would go, suspend herself over nothing, risk it all. One. She held the breath in as long as she was able. Two. Leap!

She stretched across the gap and could see the goats far below, and the ocean and the sand, and for one brief moment she wondered if those faraway figures would be rushing up to meet her. Then, however, her fingers grasped the edge, and dust and pebbles skittered away from where they dug into the rock. She kicked against the wall in front of her, tried to pull up, and slipped back. Her fingers hurt. She tried to kick one leg up to the side and catch it on the ledge but nearly lost her grip altogether. Her fingers slid. A bare lip of rock remained, cutting into her fingers. She thought she couldn't hold on anymore, but she knew she had to try so she swung one more time with all her strength, trying to get just one leg over the edge. And, at last, she did it. She pulled herself over the lip of the edge and lay on her back, chest heaving. This process repeated itself several times, until, finally, she neared the top of the spire.

She reached the top before Burgess, and she was lying there catching her breath when she heard tiny hooves hit nearby. She scrambled to her feet. Burgess stood in front of her, his horns lowered. She pointed at the goat and said, "I hope this proves to you I'm not a servant of the Blight."

"Oh, I knew that already, Paladin."

Validus gasped. She hadn't told the goats she was the paladin. Even Randull called her a relative of the paladin. "How did you know?"

Burgess slapped one hoof against the rock and lowered his horns toward her in a menacing way. "Because. *I'm* a servant of the Blight."

Chapter Ten

SERVANTS OF THE BLIGHT

Validus stepped back, suddenly aware she was too close to the edge. In front of her stood Burgess, the goat who claimed to be a servant of the Blight. She tried to move along the edge of the drop-off, toward a safer place. But the area at the top of the spire was small, and Validus didn't know what she would do if the goat made a sudden lunge for her. She considered trying to climb back down, but she knew the goat would be faster and on more solid footing.

A strong breeze blew against her, but it wasn't like the mad winds in the Passage—it was that gentle voice which had spoken to her in the principal's office. "Be strong," the voice said. "You are the paladin! Take courage!" Validus nodded and hope flooded her heart. She crouched, getting ready for the goat's attack.

Burgess watched her with his unblinking yellow eyes, his horns lowered. His hooves pawed the ground. "The grumbacher sent word to me," he said. "He told me you were coming and described what you looked like. He said to keep you busy for a short time because he was almost back to his old self and he would see you soon."

Validus scanned the ground for a rock or a stick or anything she could use to defend herself. "I don't plan to see him ever again," Validus said. Burgess rushed at her, and she managed to quickly step aside as his heavy horns steered toward her knees. His face hung over the edge of the cliff before he swung back to look at her and snorted.

Validus could see the goats far below, watching to see who would be victorious in the contest to climb to the top. Surely they saw something was wrong by now. She hoped they were preparing to leap up the side of the spire to rescue her.

"Why would you serve the Blight, anyway, Burgess? It's the enemy of life, the destroyer of every good thing!"

"No. The Blight promised to leave me as the ruler of Blaggard's Rock. I'll be the king of the goats. You're the only thing in my way. The Blight wants you dead."

Validus felt a glimmer of hope. If the Blight wanted her dead, it must be afraid of her. It was strange, she thought, that the death threat of an alien force could make her hopeful. "Why does it want me dead?"

"Because you're the paladin. Only a paladin could stop Silverback and his Breakers from getting into the Locked World."

Validus stood up straight. "That's right. I'm the paladin of Earth and the defender of six worlds. And I'm not going to let one little goat get in my way."

He snorted. "What are you going to do? Hit me with a stick?" He leapt toward her again, and this time she stepped aside and simultaneously kicked him hard, her foot swinging up and catching him in the side. He flew a few feet and landed on his side. He jumped up and immediately charged her again, but this time she was too slow, and his horns caught her left leg and sent her spinning for the edge. She slipped off the side and reached out to grab the lip.

Her shirt caught on a small outcropping of rock. She quickly reached up to pull herself back on the top of the spire and was surprised when her fingers touched it. It was almost sticky. It was easy to grab, easy to hold, and she found it almost simple to pull herself back up. She stood at the top, and although her leg was throbbing where the goat had rammed her, she was ready to fight.

The goat backed up to the far edge of the rock and got ready to charge. Validus readied herself, wondering whether she could kick him again or if she'd find herself on her second—and final—trip over the side of the cliff. The goat leapt across the space between them, and just as she prepared to sidestep it, a wall of stone appeared between them. The goat hit the wall and fell to the side.

The goat shook his head and dragged himself back to his feet. "I don't know how you did that," he said, "and I don't care. Soon you'll be at the bottom of the spire, your body broken into little tiny pieces. Just like the Sword of Six Worlds."

But even as Burgess said this, a hand made of stone and twice as big as the goat, came out of the ground and picked him up like a child holding a chick. Burgess struggled and yelled but couldn't free himself from the giant hand. Validus kept her distance, not sure what this strange new thing could be. But then a hole opened in the ground, and she could see a long stairway. A few small, floating lights came out, followed closely by Alex.

"Hiya, old buddy old pal," said Alex, but before he could say anything more Validus wrapped him in a giant hug.

"Are you okay, what happened, and how did you come out of the ground, and did you do something to that goat?"

"Slow down, Val. My friend Pookie happened to the goat."

"Is that the name of those floating lights? Pookie?"

"No, Pookie's the— Well, I don't know the right thing to say. He's like a man made out of rock. See him down there in the tunnel?"

"No, I just see a long flight of stairs."

"Weird. I'll introduce you guys later, I guess. But right now we should get downstairs with this traitor and see if we can get any information. Pookie says the Breakers are getting closer to their goal and we have to hurry."

Validus stepped down into the stairway, and a few of the bobbing lights flew ahead of her, brightening the way. "Those things are amazing, Alex!"

"They're Pookie's pets." Alex paused at the top of the stairs, framed in the light from outside. He looked back at the goat. "I'm not sure the best way to take the talking goat downstairs. You know there are talking animals here, right?"

Validus stopped. "You know that Ben and Apul are talking animals here, too, right?"

"What?"

"Apul is a horse, and Ben is a tiger."

"That's weird."

"Yeah."

Alex laughed. "And I can talk to rocks, and you're the Earth's last hope, O Mighty Paladin." Burgess bleated in outrage, and Alex took another look at him. "I think if we do this right, the hand could just walk down with the goat. What do you think, Pookie?" Alex turned and looked toward the wall, his head cocked as he listened. "Oh, that's a much better idea. Let's do that."

"Who are you talking to?"

"Pookie, of course."

"And who is Pookie again?"

"It's a long story. He's a multidimensional rock. He suggested I just let the goat into the passageway, close it behind him, and then keep collapsing it so he's forced down the stairs. I think we should run ahead of him a little ways, though, so he doesn't give us a head-butt." He and Validus ran down the stairs, and then she watched in wonder as the stone hand pushed the goat into the passageway, which immediately closed up behind him. The bobbing lights lit the way far ahead of the near total darkness that came as soon as the entrance closed.

The trip down was much faster with stairs, although Validus wasn't particularly fond of the dark or the murmurs and bleating coming from behind them. On the other hand, it was a great pleasure to be with Alex again. The whole thing suddenly seemed easier—still crazy, of course—but at least she would try to save the world with a good friend instead of alone.

The stairs ended against a stone wall, and Alex smiled apologetically in the dark. "Just a minute. Pookie is making sure this place won't collapse if I open a door here."

He put his hand on the wall, and it melted away to reveal sunlight, the beach, and the waves. And a circle of angry goats.

Randull stepped up first. He looked at Validus and then Alex with yellow eyes. "What's going on here?"

Validus stepped out of the way, and Burgess came trotting out of the tunnel, which smoothly returned to its original rock face. Burgess immediately shouted, "She's a servant of the Blight, and so is this boy!"

"I made it to the top first," Validus said.

"Because I gave her a head start."

One of the older goats called out, "Where did you find this rock mage?"

"Rock mage?"

"I think he's talking about you, Alex."

"Oh. I'm a friend of Validus's. I didn't know I was a, uh, rock mage until I came here. None of the rocks talk where I come from."

"They're traitors!" Burgess shouted again. "Traitors and servants of the Blight!"

Validus threw her hands up in frustration. "On top of the spire, Burgess told me he is a servant of the Blight, but no one was there to hear it."

"I think we should take this to the Council," said one of the goats. "Clearly someone is a traitor, and the Council needs to know there's a servant of the Blight in the Citadel."

A young goat came running up, bleating. "Yorrick's here with one of the Peers!"

"That should clear things up," Randull said. They all turned to look in time to see the chubby armadillo making his way hurriedly across the sand, followed closely by a man with silver hair and a dark beard who was dressed in a dark blue robe.

"Oh dear," Yorrick called, long before he was close enough to talk to them normally. And he kept saying it until he was standing in front of them, out of breath and huffing. He bowed to Validus several times. "My dear lady," he said, "when you said you were a kid I had no idea you meant you were a *kid*. You should have said human, you know, for future reference—or even *child* could have helped avoid confusion—but as it is I've sent you to live with the goats until Ambassador Pierce here explained it all to me. And when he told me you weren't a relative of the paladin but, ulp—" He bowed again, his pointy nose touching the ground. "My sincerest regrets, Paladin."

The goats gasped. Several of them shouted, and Randull cried out, "You're a paladin? Why didn't you say something?"

Ambassador Pierce looked at Validus with a smirk in his eye. "You didn't tell them you're a paladin? Or one of the Twelve Peers?"

Validus shrugged. "I wasn't sure until recently that I am."

He put his hand on her shoulder. "Never forget who you are. It causes trouble." He looked over at Alex. "And who is this?"

"I'm Alex."

"Ambassador Pierce. And how did you get past the Citadel's security, Alex?"

Alex shrugged. "I didn't run across any."

Burgess blew a raspberry. "He burrowed through the ground like a rabbit."

Ambassador Pierce regarded Alex carefully. "Could it be you are a rock mage? It's been a hundred years since there was a rock mage on this world. And much, much longer on our own world."

"You're from Earth, then?"

"Of course. We exchange ambassadors with five of our adjoining worlds, and a few that are secondary and even tertiary connections. They've sent their ambassadors to us as well."

Validus snickered. "Do you mean somewhere on Earth there's a talking animal representing the Citadel?"

"That's precisely what I mean. He's a fat, well-cared-for cat named Phinneas Falbrook the Third. He lives in an apartment in New York City with an old woman who has no idea he can talk. She calls him Fuzzywoogims."

Randull cleared his throat. "The real problem, sir, is that Burgess here appears to be a servant of the Blight."

Yorrick shrieked so loudly everyone jumped. "A traitor! Mannin, write this down immediately! We will need a jail cell, suitable for a goat. Mannin? Where is that rat when I need him?"

"We must take him to the Council immediately. Paladin Smith and the rock mage will come with us. Randull, choose four goats to guard Burgess." The ambassador looked sadly at Burgess. "I don't know what they promised you, Burgess, but it pains me to see you betray the good people of the Citadel."

Burgess gave the ambassador a doleful stare. "I may still have a chance, Ambassador. Silverback will break into the Locked World at any moment, I can feel it."

"All the more reason for us to make haste. Come along, everyone." The ambassador led them all along the beach and toward the exit. Validus and Alex exchanged glances and followed.

"Didja hear that, Val? Rock mages are special. One in a million. You paladins are a dime a dozen."

Validus smiled at him. She didn't want to fight. She didn't even want to pretend to fight. She figured there would be plenty of fighting soon enough.

Chapter Eleven

THE COUNCIL
AT CLOUD'S PEAK

The ambassador led the troop of two humans, one armadillo, six goats, and a growing menagerie of interested animals through the busy walkways of the Citadel and then up a long, winding staircase. Burgess bleated and cried out the whole way, and Randull, who was now looked on with increased respect by the goats, occasionally shouted at the traitor to be silent.

Yorrick came scurrying in front of Ambassador Pierce. "Sir? It seems you are headed for Cloud's Peak rather than the Council chambers."

"That's correct, Yorrick. We've moved the meetings up to Cloud's Peak because the clouds wished to be at this meeting and the Council agreed this would be wise. The clouds have even gathered a quorum."

"Oh dear, I wish someone would have told me, and I would have made arrangements."

"We've no time for refreshments, Yorrick. This is a war council, and what is decided must be carried out quickly."

"Nevertheless," Yorrick said and quickly scurried away, calling back, "I'll return with refreshments!"

Alex and Validus pushed up alongside the ambassador. "Did you say the clouds will be at the Council meeting?"

The ambassador paused. "Yes, Paladin, that's correct. The clouds on this world are alive. It's an interesting phenomenon. I've not heard that our explorers have found anything like it on other worlds, though there is one adjacent world they may have migrated from." He turned to Alex. "The clouds gain in intelligence as more of them gather. I suppose for this gathering, the clouds will be rather dense. They'll likely be dark, foreboding, and frightening. But it's only because they're packed in so closely to Cloud's Peak."

Validus elbowed Alex in the side. "Don't you want to ask about being a rock star or whatever it is?"

Alex shrugged. "Rock mage. I already talked it over with Pookie. He agrees it's likely, but he didn't know the word people use for it here."

"What does it mean, exactly? That you can control rocks?"

"Not control them, just talk to them. If they're friendly they may do what a rock mage asks. The rocks here are friendly. See?" He pointed down at the step in front of Validus, and it suddenly took on the shape of a face pointing its tongue out at Validus. Then it smoothed out into a stone again. Alex laughed.

"Very funny, Alex."

"I thought so. And so did the steps."

"Me, too," Randull said. There was bleating from behind him again, and he shouted, "Quiet, traitor!"

They came at last to a large chamber with thick carpets throughout. The walls were stone, and on the far side stood an enormous stone door, ornately carved. A giant ruby, the size of the world globe in their classroom back home, was set in the center of the door.

The ambassador turned to look at his entourage. "Here we are. It's going to be cold out there and quite possibly wet. Keep close, and unless someone on the Council speaks to you, keep your mouths shut. Don't let the prisoner wander off either; the Council will want words with him."

Ambassador Pierce walked up to the ruby and said loudly, "This is Ambassador Pierce, of the Twelve Peers of Earth, together with Paladin Validus Smith, also of the Twelve Peers of Earth, and our guests." The ruby glowed, and then the door melted away.

The wind whipped in around them, immediately reminding Validus of the Passage of the Winds. She shivered. The ambassador walked out first, his robes flapping around him, and Validus and Alex came close behind.

The room known as Cloud's Peak was not a room at all but a large, tiled, flat spot near the top of the Citadel. The floor was level, and the tiles were various shades of blue, black, and white, spraying out in beautiful geometric arrangements all the way to the edges of the room. It was about the size of a football field. Validus felt more relaxed at once when she saw that. Black clouds filled the sky as far as Validus could see, and lightning jumped from cloud to cloud. Near the center of the room stood a circle of various types of chairs and perches. The ambassador walked up to it without hesitation and bowed his head slightly as he approached.

A giant bird on a large perch turned his eyes on the ambassador and said, "We recognize you, Ambassador Pierce of Earth, and it is our pleasure to meet your new paladin. We have heard a great deal about you, Paladin." The bird turned its head to nod at two human-sized chairs, both with arms and high backs. When he turned his head Validus saw a long, vivid crack in his beak. It was the biggest bird she had ever seen. She thought it might be a condor. The ambassador took his seat and motioned for Validus to take the one next to him. Alex came up behind her chair and stood at her right hand.

Around the circle sat a variety of animals. On Crackbeak's left was an ox. The ox stood rather than sat, and perched on his shoulder was a mouse who wore a splendid green robe. A monkey with a crest of yellow fur on his face sat sprawled in a tiny chair, and next to him sat a tall rooster—nearly as tall as the wolf beside the rooster. The wolf had only one eye and multiple places where his fur was torn out, revealing white scars beneath. An iguana perched on a curve of wood. Then there was an old, gray goat and a pig beside a black horse. Lastly, Benjamin sat on her haunches between the horse and Crackbeak. She grinned when Validus saw her.

"The question remains," old Crackbeak said, "what is our best course of action? We know Silverback's Breakers are on the verge of opening the Locked World. There is precious little time for talk. The time has come for action."

Ambassador Pierce raised his hand, and Crackbeak gave him permission to speak. "This Council has already received news regarding Paladin Smith and her journey, but in the short time since she arrived she has also uncovered a servant of the Blight here in this Citadel." A chorus of squawks, grunts, barks, growls, and yips rang out in response to this news, and an arc of lightning sped through the clouds above, followed by a monstrous, rumbling peal of thunder, which shook Cloud's Peak. Randull pushed Burgess into the center of the Council.

"Shame!" shouted the pig.

"This can't be true," said the monkey. "We can't condemn this fellow without proof."

"Oh, it's true," Burgess said, and a sly look came across his face. "Silverback approached me three years ago."

A heavy wind blew across the room, and Validus thought she heard a whisper in it. She sat forward in her chair and leaned over to Alex. "Did you hear that?"

"Yeah, three years. Wow."

"No, the wind."

Alex looked at her strangely. "Sure, I heard the wind."

"Did you hear it . . . talking?"

Alex laughed. "I talk to rocks, not the wind, Val."

The wind blew again, and she heard a small whisper but couldn't make out the words.

Burgess said, "The Breakers will open the Locked World within ten hours. That's not even long enough for you to march an army there, Crackbeak."

The wolf growled and jumped to his feet. "You will refer to Councillor Crackbeak with the proper respect, or I will tear your throat out."

"No need for that sort of talk, Ralna," said the iguana slowly. "This is our only avenue to communicate with the Breakers."

Ralna settled back to his sitting position but reluctantly.

Crackbeak said, "Burgess, tell your Breakers if they surrender now, we will be lenient with those who have followed Silverback. He and the other leaders, of course, must be punished for the murders and other crimes they have committed, but we will be merciful to those who were not involved in such things."

Burgess laughed. "The Breakers will show you no such mercy, Crackbeak. When the forces of the Blight break through into this world, they will march to the Citadel and take you captive. They will force you into the Locked World, and you, too, will become a servant of the Blight. You will march together with us on this entire world." He laughed again. "I will ask Silverback to have you as my own servant," he said to Ralna, who growled but did not stand up again.

"How can he possibly know how close the Breakers are to their goal?" the rooster asked. "It takes hours to send even swift messengers between there and here. Either Burgess is lying to us—which seems likely given his allegiances—or the last messages he received are out of date and the Locked World is open already!"

Burgess laughed. "Fools. Silverback is speaking to me even now. And he has told me, as a show of his power, it is time for me to escape here."

"Don't be ridiculous," the ox laughed. "You wouldn't make it a hundred steps before a tiger and a wolf had you by the scruff of your neck."

"Or a monkey!" shouted the monkey.

The ox laughed. "That goes without saying, of course."

The wind blew again, but many on the Council were laughing now, and Validus jumped to her feet. "He is speaking to the Breakers. A mad wind is whispering in his ears."

Benjamin's ears perked up. "Validus, are you certain?"

"I can hear them but not make out the words."

Burgess looked stealthily from face to face and then, unexpectedly, began running for the edge of the room. "Block the door," Ralna snapped, and Randull and his goats immediately trotted over and set up a semi-circle of horns in front of the door.

Benjamin and Validus had both jumped up from their spots on the circle and chased the goat. He exited the circle on Val's side so she had an advantage, and she leapt after the furry form and grabbed hold of his pelt. He paused only long enough to butt her, and she tumbled to the side.

Alex yelled, "Stop him!" and the ground around the goat buckled, the colored tiles falling away as giant stone hands came up from the ground, grasping at the goat. Benjamin bounced from one granite hand to the other and took a dive straight for the goat's back, but the goat turned abruptly, and she landed beside him.

A bolt of lightning scarred the ground where the goat had just been, but Burgess was nearly to the edge of the platform now. The goat gave out one victorious cry and leaped off the side of the Citadel. Benjamin jumped for him, missed, and tried to skid to a stop before reaching the edge. Her paws scrambled for purchase, slipped, and she dropped off the side of the building.

The wind picked up, and Burgess lifted gracefully into the air. As it whipped him away, he shouted, "If you run a white flag of surrender in this room, perhaps Silverback will show *you* mercy when his army comes." Crackbeak spread his great wings and leaped into the air after him, but a massive crosswind came and drove him into the ruby gem in the center of the Citadel's door. He crumpled to the ground, and enraged thunder boomed across the valley as the clouds fired lightning at the escaping goat.

Validus stood at the edge of the room, gasping for breath and shouting Benjamin's name. Alex came up beside her. "It's okay, Val. I got her." A stone hand came up over the side and gently set the tiger back into Cloud's Peak.

"That was a near thing," Benjamin said. "Thank you, Alex."

"Crackbeak is unconscious," the pig cried.

The door dissolved beside him, and there stood Yorrick with a giant tray of food. "Refreshments, anyone?"

"Not now, you silly beast!" The pig knocked the food onto the ground and pulled Crackbeak onto the tray. "To the infirmary!" The pig sped away, with the armadillo waddling along behind him.

Validus turned around and looked at what remained of the assembled animals. "Listen to me. I am the only paladin you have right now. I will take a small group to the site of the Breakers. We will stop the Breakers or, failing that, at least slow them down."

"You'll never get there in time," said the mouse. "We would be wiser to prepare the Citadel for their assault."

"I can get us there quickly," Alex said. "I'm not sure how it works, but Pookie says by jumping through a few of his dimensional cracks we might get there faster than Burgess."

"I'll come with you," Ralna said.

"No," Benjamin said gently. "You'll be needed here, in case we fail. Gather our armies, Ralna."

He bowed his head. "You are right." He trotted to the goats. "You followed orders quickly and well a moment ago. Come with me, and we will prepare our army for a siege."

"Sir, with your permission, I will join the paladin."

"Granted, Randull. Fight bravely." Ralna turned and nodded at Validus, and then he and the goats trotted into the Citadel.

Thunder rumbled and Benjamin said, "A tribe of clouds near the Breakers is changing course to join us."

"Us?"

"Yes, Validus, I am going with you and Alex. And Randull."

Randull spit in disgust. "I don't want some girl with crippled hooves saving the day alone."

Apul appeared at the door to Cloud's Peak and came over to them. "Ralna sent me to join you."

Val smiled at him. "Alex, how do we get started?"

Alex closed his eyes, and a pained look crossed his face. "Just a minute, Val." Sweat popped out on his forehead, and he groaned as a large hole opened in the ground ahead of them, spinning like a whirlpool. Chunks of tile broke off and fell into the center, and

Val didn't hear them hit the ground inside. "It's like a slide," Alex said, his eyes still closed. "It's . . . safe. Mostly. And fast."

"Good enough for me," Randull said, and with a goat war cry he jumped in. Validus could hear his exuberant cheer for a long time before it faded. It sounded like he was having the time of his life, like he was on a waterslide. Benjamin jumped in next, followed by Apul.

"I have to go last," Alex said, and Validus realized she had been standing at the edge—looking down into the strange, smooth, flashing, spinning tunnel—and she had no intention of jumping. Then the ground disappeared beneath her feet, and she was flying down a tunnel much, much faster than any waterslide she had ever seen.

Chapter Twelve

THE PALADIN
IN CHAINS

The tunnel Alex created felt like a water-slide in one sense. It was fast—so fast Validus could barely get a breath to scream. But it was steeper than any waterslide because she was falling almost straight down. And it twisted. She spun in freefall, and the colors in the tunnel flickered past her for a long time. Eventually, though, the incline decreased, and soon Validus could tell for sure she was slowing. There was one last dip, and she shot up a smooth ramp and landed on her rear in a big stone room. She bumped to a stop, her clothes disheveled, her feet above her head, and her hair in her face.

"Very dignified," Apul said, and Benjamin and Randull laughed.

"I suppose you three all landed on your feet?"

Benjamin grinned. "I'm a cat, dear."

Val stood and rearranged herself. They waited a few minutes, but Alex didn't come bumping along after her. "He was right behind me."

Apul snorted. "Wonderful. We'll be trapped underground while the Blight destroys all life up above. What a terrible way to die."

"Shush," Benjamin said.

The room was large and well lit, with a ceiling about twenty feet above them. They spread out and started looking around, being careful not to step too near the tunnel they had come in through. Randull trotted back from the farther recesses of the room. "I found some little bobbing lights. And some sort of map."

They followed him and came to a large stone tray, set at about the height of a dinner table. Validus looked at it and could see it was a topographical map. It had some low hills and a shaft going under one of them. Small rocks moved around on the map, and when she looked closer she could see they were in the shapes of different animals. While they watched, a tiny piece of quartz shaped like a gorilla popped into the map, moving around the outskirts of a large group of animals.

"Silverback," Benjamin said.

Validus bent closer to see a small representation of what looked like a human woman, chained to a post. And next to her, also chained, was a rabbit. On a pedestal near them was a broken sword. Apul gasped. "The paladins! So they're still alive!"

"Your paladin is a rabbit?"

"Yours is a child," Apul pointed out reasonably.

Randull looked back out into the main part of the room. "Someone is coming through that tunnel." Validus turned. Alex came flying out of the tunnel, tucked into a ball. He put his arms out first and then his feet, and he landed perfectly.

"Bravo!" Apul said, and Alex took a bow, smiling.

"I landed perfectly," Validus said to Alex.

He grinned. "Pookie told me all about it while I was scouting out the Breaker camp."

"Is that what this tray is?"

Alex walked up beside her. "Yes. I had to get a little closer to set the map. It should update by itself now. See?" The little rocks were moving around. A long line of them went in and out of the shaft under the hill, like ants. He pointed at the quartz gorilla. "That's Silverback, or so Pookie said. And look, there's the Sword of Six Worlds. Silverback has it on display, to show everyone how he broke it. And this," he pointed at the two paladins chained to the post. "One is the paladin of this world. A rabbit. The other is *our* old paladin, Val. It's *Miss Holly*."

Val's eyes flew open. "Miss Holly our teacher?"

"Yeah. I tried talking to their chains because they're metal, but Pookie said they're from another world. He called it a dead world. He said nothing from there can speak at all."

Validus leaned over the map. She pointed at the mineshaft. "And this mineshaft is where the Locked World is?"

Alex shrugged. "We think so. There's a sort of sick rock surrounding it, which Pookie says is probably because it's so close to breaking open. I can't see it through the stone. So we'll have to go in and see it with our own two eyes if we want a look in there."

"That's the most important place to see."

"We should disguise ourselves and try to get in," Apul said.

Val tapped her fingers against her teeth. "I think, first, we try to get Miss Holly and that rabbit free."

"His name is Kirrik."

"Kirrik, then."

"We're here to stop the Blight, not set the paladins free. The Breakers could open the Locked World at any moment."

Val looked at Apul before she spoke. "True. But Miss Holly and Kirrik might know something we don't. If we can get them down here, maybe we'll learn something important."

Apul looked beseechingly at Benjamin. "Tell her this is a bad idea."

Benjamin licked her chops. "She's the paladin, Apul. We should follow her advice."

"She's not even trained."

"She's doing fine," Benjamin said. She turned her green eyes back to Validus. "So what do we do first?"

"Alex, can you get me up there next to Miss Holly without anyone seeing me?"

"No problem." A stairway lifted from the ground and wound along a thick column up into the ceiling. Alex led the way, and Validus came up the stairs just behind him. He pointed to a small shelf at the top. "Lie down on this, and I'll push you through the stone and onto the ground beside her. I'll keep a close watch on the map to make sure no one's watching. Go anywhere you like other than the mineshaft. If you get in trouble, I'll pull you back in here."

A sudden thought occurred to her. "Could we just pull Miss Holly and Kirrik down here?"

He shook his head. "Those dead world chains. I can't get them to move. Pookie says they're magic. They would choke to death before I could get them down here." He thought a moment more. "I could put a stone room around them, Val. Then we'd have plenty of time to figure out how to get them out and to talk to them."

"But Silverback and the Breakers would know we're here."

"Right."

"Okay, then. Stick to the plan." Alex nodded and headed down the stairway. She could hear the others talking by the map, and Alex started to give her updates on whether anyone was near the paladins above her.

Then he shouted, "Here we go!" Her shelf pushed up and out, and she was lying on the ground beside Miss Holly, who jumped and nearly cried out.

"Validus? Is that you?"

Miss Holly's face was bruised, and she was lying on her side, her hair matted and bloody. She was wearing a green tunic with a silver sword on the front, a golden sun on one side of the hilt, and a slivered moon on the other. The rabbit wasn't moving at all, except for shallow breathing. His eyes were closed.

"Yes," Validus said. "I've come to rescue you. And Kirrik. And to stop the Breakers."

Miss Holly smiled, but Val could tell it hurt her. "I knew you would make an excellent paladin, Validus."

"Alex is with me too. Is there anything you know that might help us?" From where she was laying, Validus couldn't see everything around her, but she knew Miss Holly and Kirrik's bodies should be shielding her from sight unless someone walked directly up to them. "How did they catch you? How did they break the Sword of Six Worlds? And how did I become paladin? This wind spoke to me and told me I was the paladin, but everyone seems to think there can only be one at a time and that you must be dead. But you're not."

Another pained look shot across Miss Holly's face. "I'm glad he spoke to you, Validus. That's a voice from the Architect, who built all the gateways between our worlds. He can speak to the paladins, or any of the peers, when he thinks it's useful. I'm not the paladin any longer for the same reason the sword is broken."

Miss Holly tried to turn to look over her shoulder, but she couldn't move well. "I have to tell you the secret of the sword, Validus. It's designed to destroy creatures of the Blight. It's a special sword, and it has the power not only to cut like an ordinary sword but also to give deep insights into your enemies. It can do other things, too, that will require training. It's one of the most powerful weapons in all the worlds I've been to. But there's one rule. It must only be used on a living being when you feel *compassion* for them, with one exception: creatures actually infected with the Blight."

"Like grumbachers, things like that?"

Miss Holly's eyes widened. "You saw a grumbacher?"

Validus nodded, but there was no time to share her story. "So, to use the sword you need to feel compassion for whoever you use it on. You mean, like, I have to feel sorry for them?"

"Sort of. Compassion is when you see someone hurting, for instance, and you hurt so badly for them it makes you sick, and you want to take the hurt away."

"How could anyone feel that way about Silverback? He's trying to kill us all, and when he's done here, he wants to do the same thing to Earth. And look what he's done to you! And he sent that horrible grumbacher after us." Validus could feel her anger growing. If her dad were here, he would tell her to take a deep breath and try to relax, but he wasn't here, and that was the fault of the Blight too. She shouldn't have to be on some strange world fighting evil. She should be back home telling her parents she didn't want to do the dishes.

Miss Holly coughed for a minute, and her eyes were filled with concern. "The grumbacher was chasing you? Are you all right?"

"It's still out there somewhere. I guess all that about the sword doesn't matter now that it's broken." Validus heard someone speaking near them, and she lay still, hoping Alex didn't drop her back into the cave.

"You don't understand," Miss Holly whispered. "The sword broke because I used it in anger. Silverback killed a paladin from another world. He grabbed him by the stalk—he was a plant—and broke him in half. I was so angry that I swung with all my might and broke the sword against him. *I* broke the sword. And that's when I stopped being the paladin. It's a rule that cannot be ignored."

"It doesn't matter now," Validus said.

Miss Holly reached out with one hand, the shackles clanking loudly when she moved them. "It does matter, Val. If I could have used that sword against Silverback . . . if I could have done it with compassion in my heart . . . we would have beaten him, I'm sure of it."

"It's too late now, though," Val said, and even as she spoke another, whispered voice said, "It's not too late."

"He's speaking to you," Miss Holly said. "The Architect. Tell him I'm sorry."

"It's not too late," the voice said. "Take hold of the sword, and I will repair it. And tell Holly that I can hear her."

"He can still hear you," Validus whispered. "I have to go now. I'll come back when I can, to free you both." She propped herself up on one elbow and looked over Miss Holly's side. She could see Silverback standing nearby, his wide back turned toward her. She could see the massive gorilla muscles under his fur, and she wondered how she would dare to get close enough to him even if she had the sword.

"Be careful," Miss Holly whispered.

Validus nodded and moved quickly toward the pedestal with the broken pieces of the sword on it. She ducked behind a rock about halfway there when she heard a shrill yell from beyond the ape. It was someone shouting, "Intruder!"

She jumped up and saw Burgess, a look of triumph on his face, shouting "intruder" over and over. Silverback had already turned and seen her, and he loped toward her, his long ape arms stretching out ahead of him. He covered the distance between them fast, his fangs bared and dark eyes terrifying. Miss Holly shouted at her to run, and she dashed for the sword. She was nearly there, but she looked back. The ape bore down on her. She would never make it in time, he was too close. She screamed for Alex, and the ground opened in front of her. She jumped feet first into the hole, and she could tell by the shadow above her the ground was closing in over her head.

But at the last moment a long, furred arm snatched her by the neck and pulled her up out of the cave. The ground closed up beneath her feet, and the ape held her up to his face and shook her. "Hello, little girl," he said. "Welcome to the Breakers."

Chapter Thirteen

SILVERBACK'S STORY

Nearly the same moment Silverback grabbed hold of Validus, Alex sent stone warriors up out of the ground to fight the ape. Silverback laughed and held Validus up. "There's a rock mage around, it seems. If I see any sign of you again, mage, I break this girl in half." The stone men hesitated then melted back into the ground.

"You have powerful friends," the ape said. He held her close to his hairy face. "But soon I'll be more powerful. You had best make friends with *me*."

"I never said I wasn't your friend."

"Ha. Yes. A baby paladin who wants to be my friend. Right, Burgess?"

The goat laughed too. "She's not *my* friend."

Silverback looked at her carefully and then snapped at Burgess to bring him some chain. "You're just a baby paladin. What did they tell you about me, baby Paladin?"

"That you're an evil, twisted creature who wants to let the Locked Worlds free to kill this world."

Silverback looked pained. "They're wrong, you know. The Locked Worlds were locked only because of someone called the Architect. He thinks he's in charge of all the worlds because he built us these gateways. He hates the Blight—of course they don't call themselves the Blight—and he's purposely told lies about them to shut them out of various worlds. Did you know the Blight never gives their gifts to anyone without permission? It's true. And they coexist in many worlds in perfect harmony with the people and animals who live there. Ask your Architect about that!"

Validus listened for the whispered voice of the Architect, but there was nothing.

"Not talking to you now, is he?" The ape laughed. "I'll tell you my story," he said. "And then you can see if you think I'm evil or not."

Miss Holly cried out, "Validus! Don't listen to him! He tells lies. He'll try to convince you to help the Breakers."

Silverback grinned. "It's true, baby Paladin. If you listen to my story, I'll try to convince you to help me."

Validus hesitated. Seeing Miss Holly's bruised and bloodied face reminded her how serious this whole thing was, and she felt a flash of anger. Her father always told her that the best decisions were made with the best information. "I'll hear what you have to say."

"You don't have any choice," he said, laughing again.

Burgess came up with a long length of chain and a stake, and Silverback snapped two manacles in place on her wrists. He took the slack of the chain and staked it into the ground. She looked at the length of the chain.

It looked like it might reach all the way to the sword's pedestal, if only she could distract the ape somehow.

"Validus, I'm begging you not to listen to him."

Silverback grunted. "Bring a gag for the failed paladin." Apparently Burgess had already thought of this because two squirrels came bounding up behind him and tied a rag into Miss Holly's mouth.

"My father was one of the Twelve Peers here on this world," Silverback said. "He was the Plenipotentiary. Some would say the most powerful of the Peers." Silverback grunted. "He wasn't easy to please at home. He demanded the best from everyone around him. I could never please him. I never particularly liked him. I loved him, of course, as only a son can love a distant father.

"My mother was my greatest friend. She believed in me. And when Father became angry at me, she was the one to take me aside and stroke my fur and tell me all would be well."

Validus shifted the manacles on her wrists. "She sounds kind."

"Yes."

"What does she think of you breaking into the Locked Worlds?"

Silverback bared his fangs at her. "Wait for the story's end, Paladin. You'll know the answer to that soon enough. One day during my third summer, my parents and I and a whole band of us went down to play near the river. Most of the adults were lounging in the shade, and we children were playing in the water. We were told to stay close to the bank because of the speed of the current farther out, but I was always a strong swimmer, and one of the other children dared me to swim across to the other side. I thought this would impress my father. No other young gorilla could do it, and, as I said, I was strong.

"So I began to swim. I swam out farther than the boundary our parents had set for us without any trouble. And then I swam some distance beyond that, and my friends started calling me back. I knew I could make it so I swam farther. The current grew more difficult, but I kept going. A branch came downstream and knocked into me, but I kept going until I couldn't any longer, and the river pushed me under and downstream."

Despite her danger and all the other things going on, Validus leaned forward and grabbed his furred forearm. "How did you get out?"

"My mother. She heard the cries of my playmates and came running to the water's edge. When she saw what had happened, she and my father both ran downstream. I was going so fast they could barely catch up, and at last my mother, against my father's express commands, jumped into the river herself. She swam downstream to me and caught up just as I entered the rapids above the waterfall. My head hit a rock and blood filled the water. She wrapped one arm around me and tried to swim out, but now the current was too much for her, even without a barely conscious son in her arm.

I tried to help, but I was so weak. Because my mother slowed us down, my father managed not only to catch up with us but also to break off a large branch of a tree. He found a place where another tree hung out over the rapids, and he hurried up the tree and dangled the branch down to us.

"My mother missed the branch, but I managed to grab it, and I knew I must use all my strength to hold it no matter the cost. Our combined weight was more than the tree my father hung from could handle, and he began shouting for us to make our way to the side if we could. The branch he was on began to break. He tried to scramble backward, and my mother said that she loved me. I looked back into her eyes, and she smiled at me—a sad, tired smile. She told me again that she loved me, and she loved my father. She said we must take care of one another, and I shouted at her, 'Mother, what do you mean, what are you saying?' Then she let go."

Validus tried to say something, but the ape angrily motioned for her silence.

"Father immediately swung me to the side of the river, where I landed on the rocks at the bank, and he leaped over me and chased her downriver. I could barely stand, but I dragged myself after him. I could hear the sound of the waterfall, the deafening sound of the water crushing the rocks below, but it wasn't enough to drown out my father's shout. I came over the top of the rocks just in time to see my mother fall into the mist."

Silverback sat quietly, his eyes unfocused and staring into the distance. "My father walked past me, still carrying the soaked branch he had used to save my life and said, 'You will never be worth that sacrifice.'"

"He couldn't have meant that."

"But he did. As I said, he was a difficult person. On my tenth birthday, my nameday, he called me Silverback." He looked at Validus, and seeing she didn't understand, he said, "All apes grow a silver streak of hair on their tenth birthday. There is nothing special about it. To call an ape Silverback is the same as naming someone 'Ordinary' or 'Nothing Special.'

"I resolved to become something special. To show my father that Mother's sacrifice had been worth it. I applied to the paladin school. I was strong and smart and fast, and my father was a Peer. Everyone agreed I was a good candidate. My father showed signs of pride for the first time in my life. But then . . . the Architect didn't choose me. So I had wasted my life trying to become a paladin."

"But there were still other good things you could do—"

Silverback slapped his hand into the dirt. "But not great things. Not things that would take my common name and make it a name to be respected." He looked off at the mine. "That's when I learned about the Locked World. I came here from the Citadel, by myself, and explored the caves near here. When I entered that mine, I could hear them talking to me from the other side. They told me I could be great . . . they would make me the ruler of this world." He picked up a piece of dirt and threw it aside. "I would be more than my father ever was."

At that moment, a deep sadness fell on Validus. It had started when Silverback described his mother, but something about his driving need to be better than his father at any cost made her feel sorry for him.

A dog came running toward them from the mines. "Silverback! We've done it! We've broken through! There is something in the mine. It's asking for you."

Silverback leaped to his feet and flashed his teeth at Validus. "So you are too late, Paladin." He loped off toward the mine.

Validus slumped to the ground. She was too late. Many years too late. If only someone could have been there to help Silverback when he was young. If only someone could have told him that he was loved, that he had worth, then maybe all of this would not be happening. "Alex," she said. "The Breakers have opened the Locked World." Alex didn't answer, but a rumble of earth came from the direction of the mines. Maybe her friends were busy somewhere else.

No one was watching her, so she stood and moved toward the sword. She stretched her arms to the limit, and the tips of her fingers could just touch the hilt. Her fingers grazed it, and the hilt moved. The blade was broken into at least ten pieces. She didn't see how taking hold of the hilt would help anything, but the Architect had told her to do it. If she was only a little closer . . . .

"Hello, Miss Smith," said an unpleasant and familiar voice. Standing off to the side was Mr. Jurgins. He looked human again, except for his too-white skin and his mouth full of jagged teeth. "So nice to see you. And just when my masters are coming from underground to join us. I don't suppose they would mind if I had a little snack."

Chapter Fourteen

ALL THE LOCKS
ARE BROKEN

"Stand back!" Validus said, and Mr. Jurgins paused. "The Sword of Six Worlds is right there."

"It's broken," Jurgins said. "Broken into a dozen pieces. Besides, you can't even reach it."

"Are you certain of that? If I can, you're in trouble."

Jurgins laughed. "Oh, really? Why don't I give you a piece of the sword, just to make this whole thing more interesting. What would you like? This long piece?" He picked up a jagged shard and held it in his hand. "Or how about this little sliver? You could hold it as a knife."

"Just the hilt."

He laughed again, delighted. "I know you haven't been trained as a paladin yet, but surely you know the whole point of a sword *is* its point."

Validus did her best to look like she didn't care. A sudden chorus of screams came from the mines. "You'd better hurry if you want to kill me yourself. Sounds like your masters and the Breakers will be here soon."

Jurgins picked up the hilt and tossed it from hand to hand. "The Breakers? I doubt it. The Blight might keep its bargain with Silverback, but every other living thing in this world will become part of the Blight. It's hungry, you see, and a creature has to be quite valuable to be spared. I suppose that shouting means it has already begun. They'll be coming out of the mine soon."

He tossed the hilt to Validus, and she reached up and caught it in midair. As soon as the hilt rested completely in her palm, she felt a jolt, and a bright light came shining out of it as all the shards of the blade came flying toward her, took their place above the hilt, and, glowing white-hot, melted into place. While the sword was still burning, she struck at the dead chains, and they turned to dust with the slightest touch. She held the sword up to Mr. Jurgins, burning with anger. "Thanks for the fighting chance."

Jurgins ran. He didn't pause for a moment but bolted directly for the mine-shaft. Validus could see smoke and animals pouring from it, and the screaming was getting louder. She quickly broke Miss Holly's chains, and Kirrik's too. She pulled the gag out of Miss Holly's mouth, who took a big gulp of air.

Miss Holly's eyes filled with tears. "You did it, Validus! You're the paladin!" She looked at the reassembled sword. "But remember, Validus, don't use it in anger. I can see you're furious."

"They hurt you, Miss Holly, and a lot of other people. The Blight will destroy us all if it can. I *am* furious."

"You can't use the sword on any living thing when you have this much anger, Validus. You'll only break it again."

"Try to get Kirrik somewhere safe. If Alex can, he'll take you into the cave. I have to try to close that Locked World again." Without waiting to make sure Miss Holly had heard her, Validus ran toward the mineshaft.

She was nearly halfway there when she saw Burgess come running out, shouting, "We had a deal!" A pale white insectlike thing the size of a van came stalking out after him, and with one segmented leg it caught hold of him and dragged him back into the mine. Validus swallowed hard and kept running. Another giant insect came out of the mine and headed toward her. She wondered if she could use the sword on it because she didn't feel any compassion at all for the giant bug, only revulsion.

"It's a creature of the Blight," the Architect whispered in her ear, and Validus lifted the sword over her head and took a swipe at the bug. It fell to the side, wounded, but was still coming. She stumbled backward, and the bug loomed over her. Suddenly, a seven-foot-tall rock-man stepped between them and squashed the bug with one stony fist.

The creature's face opened, and Alex was inside it. "We had some trouble in the cave. When the Breakers opened the Locked World, Blight creatures started pouring into our cave. Pookie says it was because we were underground. We've fought them out of there now, and I've made a safe room. I've put Miss Holly and the rabbit there, and Apul is watching over them."

"Good work, Alex. Now we have to get into that mine and figure out how to close the Locked World again."

The rock armor closed over his face again, and now she noticed how the rock-man looked like Alex. "Show me the way," the rock said cheerfully.

Three more insects blocked the way to the mine now. Alex made quick work of one, crushing it with a two-handed blow, and Validus took care of another with the sword. Benjamin and Randull came up from behind them, and Randull knocked the legs out from under the third insect while Benjamin tore into its carapace. Five more came swarming at them. Benjamin yelled for Alex and Validus to get into the mine, and she and Randull would fight the bugs. They ran to the mine entrance, but just as they descended into the mine, there was a sickening crunch from behind them. Validus looked back to see Benjamin, crushed beneath a fallen bug.

"No!"

"Validus, we can't turn back, we have to focus on the task. We'll come back for her." Benjamin wasn't moving. An enormous elephant charged out of the smoke and chaos, trumpeting, and knocked into the insect on top of Benjamin.

"Ha haaaa! Never fear, Paladin! These Breakers can't treat Granger like a slave. I'll keep things under control up here. Can you believe the mad winds brought me here and made we work in these mines? Now they'll feel an elephant's wrath!"

Granger lifted the insect off Benjamin, and Randull bit the fur at the nape of her neck and pulled her out. She wasn't moving.

Alex's rock hand closed over Validus's arm. "Come on," he said. "Pookie thinks he knows how we can close the Locked World, but we have to do it quickly, before the opening gets too wide. I have to see the gap to fix it."

"But Benjamin—"

"Benjamin would tell us to close the Locked World first."

Validus tore her gaze from Benjamin, and they pushed deeper into the mine. Horrible sounds were coming from below them, the sounds of animal screams and breaking rock. At a certain point, the tunnel broke off into two directions. The sword was glowing now, and two of Pookie's floating lights slipped out of the rock and hovered near them.

"We're close, Val. Look."

A writhing army of the insectlike things gathered in the cavern ahead. Many of them had flat, wide tentacles like a grumbacher. They were pouring out of a hole the size of a house, and while hundreds were pushing out and congregating near the gap, others were moving back into the rift, carrying struggling animals in their pinchers, tentacles, or mandibles.

"Come on," Alex said, and in his stone armor he jumped down in the midst of the insects and started flattening bugs right and left. The mineshaft opened into a wide cave, a room bigger than their whole school, filled with insects, and Alex was wading through them toward the gap.

Validus went to follow him, but a large shape loomed up out of the shadows and blocked her path. It was Silverback. "I can't allow you to undo all my work, Paladin."

She pointed at the animals being forced into the gap. "Look at them screaming and trying to get away from those bugs, Silver-back," she shouted angrily. "Was that part of your deal?"

"They aren't bugs, you know. They're creatures of the Blight. Once they were like you or me, but now they are stronger and more durable than any animal in this world. I'm doing them a favor."

Validus hefted the sword, a scowl on her face. "It's time for you to step aside."

He took a step toward her, his big, leathery palm held out. "Give me the sword, baby Paladin."

"I don't want to hurt you," she said and realized at the same moment that it was true. She didn't want to hurt him. She was angry at him and furious at what he had done, but she didn't want to hurt him if she could help it.

"You can't. That sword already broke on me once." He stepped closer, a vicious grin on his face.

Validus felt her anger wavering as she remembered his story, and she wished there was some way to stop him that wouldn't involve the sword. She remembered her own father and how kind he was. She wasn't sure she had ever seen him angry, he was so calm and peaceful. And her mother, who had angry fits much like Val's, never took that anger out on her the way Silverback's father did. Her own parents seemed to have been training her from a young age to be someone important, someone special. They believed she could make a difference in the world, make it a better place, and they told her this all the time. Would things be different if Silverback's father hadn't assumed he was worthless?

She didn't want to use the sword, but Silverback was on top of her and she had no choice. She felt the last shred of her anger toward him drain away, replaced by a deep, sad regret that his actions made this necessary. "I'm sorry!" she shouted, barely able to hear her voice over the chaos of animals and blighted creatures fighting. She lifted the sword and drove it straight into Silverback's chest.

Everything went black. She couldn't see the cave or hear the sounds of the screaming or Alex fighting the Blight. She was in a completely dark room, but after a while she could hear the sound of someone crying. She followed the sound, the sword still in her hand, and she finally found the source of the crying. A baby gorilla lay crumpled in a corner, sobbing and calling for its mother. Validus set her sword down and wrapped her arms around the gorilla. "Shhh. It's okay. It's going to be okay."

"Everyone hates me," the gorilla said. "Except for my mama and she's dead."

"*I* don't hate you."

"If you knew the things I've done, you would hate me. I'm in so much trouble."

She stroked his fur. "It's okay, little friend. I know all about it. And do you know what?"

"What?"

"I still love you."

Her eyes snapped open, and the Sword of Six Worlds was humming in her hands. Silverback was lying on his back, his mouth open and eyes closed. He was still breathing, and she couldn't see a wound in his chest. The sword held no blood. Alex was fighting off the bugs, but they were swarming over him now, and he wasn't making anymore forward motion toward the gap.

Val dove into the crowd, hacking a burning trail with the sword, and she carved out a path to Alex. They worked together to make their way through the masses of blighted creatures, Alex crushing bug heads or lifting them out of the way, and Validus chopping those foolish enough to step into the gap.

Alex neared a pair of large, round stones with strange writing on them. Each stone was broken in half, and Validus knew immediately these were the seals that had kept the Locked World closed. Alex knelt and studied the broken stones and said, "We can fix this, Val. Save as many animals as you can. Get away fast. It's going to get hot."

"Alex?"

His stone armor was cracked and broken in places from the fighting. She could actually see part of Alex's arm beneath the stone casing.

"I'll be right behind you, Val."

She turned toward the line of insects that were carrying animals and hacked into them. As soon as the animals were free, they ran, flew, slithered, and hopped out of the mine as quickly as they were able. None of them stopped to help her. Alex was pushing insects back into the hole, and they didn't seem able to stop him. Validus heard a hissing sound, and the cold, biting air of the shaft suddenly turned to a heat blast and light came pouring into the room. A fountain of lava broke loose, and Alex was waving at it with his rock-encrusted hands, talking to it as it moved through the room and toward the hole.

Validus turned to look through the entrance to the Locked World. Mr. Jurgins stood on the other side, standing tall amid the flood of giant insects. He inclined his head toward Validus and smiled.

Then Jurgins leaped out of the gap and jumped on Alex's back. With swift, careful precision, he tore at the cracks in Alex's armor, and chunks of rock fell to the ground. Tentacles came out of Jurgins's side and back, and soon he was wrapped around Alex like a starfish on a rock. Alex tried to pry him off, but Jurgins couldn't be shaken. Validus ran toward them, but the heat was so powerful, she couldn't even get close. "Alex!"

He waved at her to get out. A wall of heat hit her as more lava flowed into a river toward the hole, corralling the bugs back toward the gap. The bugs hissed and clicked and tried to get out of its path, but many of them slipped into the molten rock, while others scrambled back into the Locked World. Jurgins's human face slipped. He was struggling not to shift completely to his grumbacher form.

Alex couldn't tear Jurgins off, and Validus couldn't get to them. Alex fell once and then stood and struggled to move toward

Validus. She pushed herself to go farther into the heat, but she was worried she would faint. At last Alex came within reach, and she lifted the sword to finish off Jurgins.

"You can't kill me!" he shouted at Validus and jumped away, toward the burning heat of the lava.

"If you go back inside the Locked World before we close it, I'll let you live." The Sword of Six Worlds was glowing as brightly as the lava.

"You don't understand," Jurgins said. "I mean you aren't able to kill me. Did you forget I grew back from a tentacle? Have you thought about what happened to the rest of me? I'm waiting for you back home. I wonder what the other me has done while you've been here. I hope your family is okay." He laughed, and Validus ground her teeth and charged him. Jurgins slithered backward, lost his footing, and fell into the flow of lava, a giant grin on his face.

Validus turned away before he sank completely, and she felt a knot forming in her stomach. She hoped her family was okay. She wondered what Mr. Jurgins once was, a long time ago, and whether a grumbacher could have been human before running across the Blight.

Alex lumbered toward the lava flow, shouted at her to leave the mine, and turned again toward the massive gateway into the Locked World. He waded quickly across the lava flow and up on the other side, his rock armor dripping and red-hot.

Validus made her way toward the surface, choking on the superheated air. Partway back, her foot caught on something on the cavern floor, and she stumbled, putting a hand against the wall to steady herself. It was Silverback. He hadn't moved since she left him, and his shiny face was slack, his mouth open. She could see his fangs and red tongue.

Loud noises came from behind her, and another blast of heat burst through the tunnel. She took hold of Silverback's arm to try and drag him up the tunnel, but she couldn't move him an inch. A group of animals made their way to the surface, flowing around her. She shouted at them to help her, but they took one look at Silverback and hurried on their way.

She hurried up the tunnel, looking ahead as Randull came barreling down the tunnel, a limping tiger close behind. "Benjamin!" She leaned close to Randull and shouted, "Silverback is down the tunnel, and I can't move him."

"Something is happening, Paladin," he said. "The entire tunnel is shaking. Benjamin and I came in to get you and Alex out. Where is he?"

Validus pictured Alex at the gate of the Locked World. "We can't help Alex," she said, "but we have to get Silverback out of here. Help me." Randull started to object, but Benjamin pushed past him to the fallen gorilla. She grabbed him by the back of his neck and with enormous effort began to pull him backward up the tunnel. Validus ran to the other side and pushed, and then Randull joined in, obviously still reluctant. Between the three of them, they managed to get Silverback out of the mine.

Validus put her hands on her knees, panting. The ground in front of her feet formed a face, and Alex's voice came from it. "Val, I'm losing—" He grunted as if something heavy had hit him. "I'm losing control." The stone face contorted in pain. "You need to evacuate this world. I can't lock it again. I tried. I'm sorry." His eyes closed in pain, and a low rumbling started in the mine and spread outward. The ground shook, knocking Val off her feet. The Sword of Six Worlds fell from her grip.

She picked up the sword and shouted, "Alex, I'm coming to help you!"

"You can't do anything, Val. You—" His face collapsed into pebbles.

She sped back into the mine. Black smoke pushed out the tunnel like a chimney. She ignored the heat, barely able to breathe, and ran into the cavern at the bottom of the tunnel.

Far away, across the glowing bed of lava, Alex knocked a burnt and crippled Jurgins away from him. They were both trapped by the lava, being pushed toward the Locked World. Alex stood thigh deep in the lava, but his armor was badly cracked. To go deeper risked lava seeping into his armor. Jurgins laughed and walked backward into the Locked World, taunting Alex and inviting him to come inside. Alex stood in the gate, both hands up toward the sides. He shouted, the earth rumbled and cracked, and the entire mine shook. Dust and dirt fell all around them.

Alex turned toward her and shouted. "Val, I can't do this. Jurgins came out of the lava and attacked me, and now I'm not strong enough. You need to get out." She tried to run toward him, but it was like running into an oven. She couldn't get her feet to move forward.

Alex crumpled to his knees. "Pookie says we can collapse this gate long enough to give you a chance to evacuate the Citadel, at least, but the Blight will eat through again. You have to run, Val."

The Sword of Six Worlds quivered in Validus's hand. Miss Holly said the sword could do different things depending on the paladin who uses it. Could it lock this gateway? The sword shone a whitish blue. She whispered, "Architect, please make this work."

Her sword brightened and began to vibrate so hard she thought it would fall from her hand. She took the sword and jammed the blade into the ground. A wall of light came from the sword and washed down into the mine, knocking rocks from its path. It hit Alex, and he fell in front of it. Validus cried out, but it was too late. The damage was done. The wall of energy smashed into the gateway.

The roof of the cave fell in on Alex. Val shouted for him. He disappeared in a shower of boulders from the collapsing roof. The lava splashed up over the boulders and rushed to fill the whole cave. The blue light smoothed over it all, and the sword's glow faded.

Another blast of heat came, driving Val out of the mine, and she ran back up the passageway, crying, and fell against Benjamin, wrapping her arms around her neck, the sword at their feet. The mine collapsed in a spectacular display of fire and smoke. Validus cried for a long time, and Benjamin sat beside her without saying a word.

Fires had burst out in the grass in various places, and the newly arrived tribe of clouds sent rain to put them out. Steam rose from the mine. Validus collapsed to the ground in the middle of the rain. When the tears subsided enough to talk, she said, "He did it. Alex saved us."

A hand fell on her shoulder. "*We* did it, you nut. I just supplied the lava. Jurgins would have stopped me if not for you! And you're the one who sealed the lock." She jumped up, and there Alex stood, soaked in ice cold water. "Pookie pulled me out right when the roof collapsed." But then he couldn't say anything else because the Paladin of Earth squeezed the air out of him with an enormous bear hug.

Chapter Fifteen

THE SCHOOL
IN THE SKY

The victory party . . . well, there just wasn't any way to explain it if you weren't there. It took about a week to gather up all of Silverback's Breakers, and then they had to be transported under guard to the Citadel. Citizens held a sort of pre-party when news first reached the Citadel, but when Validus and her friends arrived, the party took on new life.

An enormous celebration was arranged, which Yorrick proudly catered. Crackbeak presided over the party, mostly recovered from being slammed into the side of the Citadel by the mad winds. Benjamin and Apul sat in places of honor, and Randull was officially installed as the new leader of Blaggard's Rock, much to his pleasure. Granger received the reward of an exclusive contract for selling starflowers to the Citadel.

Validus and Alex told their story a hundred times, but it wasn't until about the eightieth that Alex admitted how scared he had been—and that the last thing Jurgins said was that he would find them again, that he would make Val and Alex pay. But even this didn't dampen the party mood because Apul, who was well known as the greatest pessimist in the Citadel, said, "He'll never find his way out from under all that lava!"

And then, at last, the day came for Alex and Val to go home. Validus didn't tell Alex that morning when she went down to see Silverback in his cell. The old ape didn't say anything to her, but he put his hand out through the bars and took her hand in his. She thought she saw a tear in his eye, but he pulled his hand back and moved away. As she walked out of the room, she heard him say something. She thought it was "thank you."

Apul acted gruff, of course, and Randull and the goats planned an elaborate ceremony, which culminated in the presentation of two thick leather gloves made to look like hooves. She pulled them over her hands, and they bleated with joy. "You're an honorary goat now," Randull said.

"A kid," she said and then laughed at the look of dismay on Yorrick's face.

It was most difficult to leave Benjamin. Validus wrapped her arms around that big orange and black neck, and Ben gently said, "You are always welcome here, Paladin." Then she licked Val with her sandpaper tongue and told them it was time for human cubs to head for home, along with Miss Holly.

Ambassador Pierce took the journey back with them. He shook Miss Holly's hand at the point of departure, the same field by which they had come into this world. The rock still stood above the grain. "Paladin, we thank you for your service," the ambassador said to Miss Holly.

"I'm not a paladin anymore."

"Never forget who you are," the ambassador said. "It causes trouble." He turned to Alex and Validus. "You have made me proud to be representing Earth to the creatures of this world." He shook each of their hands. "And I am proud to be your friend." Ambassador Pierce took a pointed white stick with brightly colored lights on it and pushed it through the air. With a pop the pointed end of the stick disappeared. He pulled it back toward him, and a hole opened in the air, just big enough for them to worm their way through.

Val looked at Alex. "Don't you want to say good-bye to Pookie?"

"Nah. He's a multidimensional rock. He's in our world too." Alex stepped through the hole first and then Val, and Miss Holly was close behind.

Validus and Alex already had created a clever story to tell their parents about where they had been, but they never asked, which was strange because they were gone for nearly two weeks. They talked about it with one another and couldn't figure it out. No one at school seemed to notice they were gone. Alex found a test in his desk from when they were missing, with his name and handwriting, though it was a lower score than he would have gotten. It was a mystery they decided to take to Miss Holly, who seemed to know something but wouldn't admit it. Another mystery was Mr. Jurgins, who was dismissed from the school after "strange behavior in the principal's office" and no one had seen him since. Validus's and Alex's families were both fine.

Now, two months later, school was out and life seemed completely normal. Val was lying on her own bed in her own room with the unicorn posters on the wall and her shoes on the bed, missing her friends in that other world and feeling, honestly, a little bored.

A sudden crack at the window startled her, and she rushed over to it to find Alex down below throwing rocks. She pushed it open. "Come in the front door, Alex! You know my mom will let you in!"

"I thought this would be more fun."

"Stop throwing rocks and get up here!"

He threw his hands up in the air. "Okay, okay, fine!"

A minute later he was in her room, and he flopped down in the chair by her door. "You've got your shoes on. Good. Now go get the sword, and put on a warm coat. I have something I want to show you."

She looked at him, confused, but he just grinned. "It's summer, Alex, why should I get a warm coat?" She got on her stomach on the floor, reached under her bed, and pulled out the sword.

"You keep the most powerful weapon in the universe *under your bed*?" Alex laughed heartily at that.

"Where else am I going to keep it? My closet? Behind the door?" She grabbed a jacket and pulled it on.

"C'mon." Alex raced down the stairs and outside, and she came behind him, strapping the sword onto her back. Miss Holly had given her a beautiful scabbard and a belt that could go around her waist or on her back.

Mrs. Smith stuck her head out the kitchen window. "Honey, are you feeling okay? I see you're wearing a coat. How's your temperature?"

"It's fine, Mom. Alex and I are just playing a game." Mr. Smith stuck his head out the window, smiled and waved absent-mindedly. Alex and Val waved back enthusiastically.

"Your parents are great," Alex said.

Validus thought about it. "Yeah, they really are, aren't they?"

Alex grinned. "I have another great thing to show you. I've been doing a little something the last couple of weeks that I think you'd like to try."

"What is it?"

"Flying."

"What?"

"Miss Holly said it's time for you to start your training so I should show you how it's done." He raised his hands straight out.

"This better not be a joke, Alex. I'll pound you."

"It's no joke. Relax." The wind was starting to blow now, hard. "Bend your knees. That's right. Now lean back and . . . jump!" He jumped backward, but before he hit the ground, the wind picked him up and he soared straight into the sky. Val lost her balance when she fell backward, but the wind picked her up, too, and she sped into the sky behind him. He laughed and called to her, and they flew up above the clouds. The sun shone spectacularly across the clouds, and Validus found she was laughing too.

"Where should we go, Alex?"

"Look around!"

She did. And then she saw it, a shining white city built on the clouds, with a castle rising up above it. Twelve brightly colored flags flew from the city walls, and she knew in an instant that this was the castle of the Twelve Peers and that she would visit often.

"Alex?"

"Yeah?"

"I'll race you!" And she dove ahead of him, toward that distant, sparkling city.

THE END

ACKNOWLEDGMENTS

Thanks to my mom and dad, who first introduced me to Narnia, Middle Earth, and the many worlds that border our own. Many, many thanks to my wife, Krista, for being a late-night sounding board and for her unwavering support of our family and my writing. Zoey, Allie, and Myca, this book would not exist if not for you three. I am proud of you and love you so much.

Thanks also to Wes Yoder for believing in Validus and her story from start to finish, and to M. S. Corley for bringing her to life for the cover.

Special thanks to my early readers: Maddie Yoder, Rachel Ronk, and Shasta Kramer.

And of course thanks to Validus Smith and Alex Shields for sitting through countless hours of interviews, answering my questions, and making sure I got the details of their story right.

Coming in 2013

THE ARMIES OF THE CRIMSON HAWK

*Book 2
in the Adventures
of Validus Smith!*

Read more at:
http://www.sixworlds.com